I0554227

JAMES ROY DALEY'S

13 DROPS OF BLOOD

BOOKS of the DEAD

This book is a work of fiction. All characters, events, dialog, and situations in this book are fictitious and any resemblance to real people or events is purely coincidental.
All rights reserved. No part of this book may be used or reproduced in any manner without written permission except in the case of reprinted excerpts for the purpose of reviews.

13 DROPS OF BLOOD

Collection copyright © 2010 by James Roy Daley

Edited by Cynthia Gould
Book Design by James Roy Daley
Cover Design by Cynthia Gould

FIRST EDITION

10 9 8 7 6 5 4 3 2 1

For more information subscribe to: booksofthedead.blogspot.com

For direct sales and inquiries contact:
besthorror@gmail.com

COPYRIGHT ACKNOWLEDGEMENTS

"The Exhibition"
Copyright 2009. First appeared in *Brutality as Art*, by Snuff Books.

"The Confession"
Copyright 2007. Original for this anthology.

"Baby"
Copyright 2010. Original for this anthology.

"A Ghost in my Room"
Copyright 2007. Original for this anthology.

"Jonathan vs. the Perfect Ten"
Copyright 2008. Original for this anthology.

"The Hanging Tree"
Copyright 2010. First appeared in *The Zombist*, by Library of the Living Dead Press.

"Thoughts of the Dead"
Copyright 2010. First appeared in *Through the Eyes of the Undead*, by Library of the Living Dead Press.

"Summer of 1816"
Copyright 2007. First appeared in *History is Dead* by Permuted Press.

"Fallen"
Copyright 2008. Original for this anthology.

"The Relation Ship"
Copyright 2006. Original for this anthology.

"Suffer Shirley Gunn"
Copyright 2008. Original for this anthology.

"Humpy and Shrivels"
Copyright 2009. Original for this anthology.

"Curse of the Blind Eel"
Copyright 2009. First published in *Dark Jesters* by Novello Publishers.

BOOKS of the DEAD

TABLE OF CONTENTS

INTRODUCTION

Dear literate horror fan—

When I started putting this collection together I figured every-thing would fall under a single, simple heading: horror. After all, I consider myself a horror writer at heart. Now, for those of you keeping score, I'm well aware that being labeled a 'horror' writer in to-day's literary world is like being labeled a 'porno' director in the film world, but I, for one, don't care. Horror is that thing I grew up on, that friend Mom says is a bad influence. Some of my earliest memories connected to the genre include me curled up in a ball, watching movies like *Jaws* or *The Omen* while my mother and father discussed whether or not I was old enough to be seeing such a thing. I remember being absolutely captivated by *'Salem's Lot* late one evening, alone in my brother's bedroom, the feeling of terror consuming me as Ben Mears and Mark Petrie made their into the basement of the Marsten house, weapons in hand, danger all around them. I could hear my family in the kitchen below—safe, secure, acting as if everything was normal in the world. For me, it wasn't. I had a pillow covering half my face, my knees were nailed to my chest, and my heart was pounding clean out of my body as the goosebumps on my arms tried to crawl from my skin and hide in the corner; I couldn't *believe* the im-ages on television could be so intolerably wrong. Who would create such a thing?

And I loved it. Oh boy, did I ever.

Strange, huh?

Well, maybe not for you. Maybe not to the people that figure reading a book called *13 Drops of Blood* is a good way to go.

Horror. I love it. And I can't imagine myself hiding behind sub-labels such as *Dark Fantasy, Dark Suspense, Visceral, Supernatural,*

Gothic, Noir, Dark Fiction, or my least favorite of all—at least when dealing with horror stories—*Speculative Fiction.* Ugh. This is where I shake my head.

For me, a horror writer hiding behind a label that's currently more accepted by the tea-sippers and the chin-strokers is a writer embracing the art of selling the reader lies. And why? Marketing? Is that the reason? Or is it to appease some eccentric echelon of self-value, to demonstrate the arc of personal growth?

It's sort of sad, really. Sad, unless of course, the writer in question believes the art falls under such a label. Then it's a different thing: to each his own. But still, something doesn't add up here. It's disappointing to watch millions of people embrace horror on the big screen, knowing that if you crack open a book the same story will be toned down and slapped with a different label... a *softer* label.

What are you reading, honey?

Who me? Oh, I'm reading a fantastic Dark Suspense novel. It's about this cannibal that owns a chainsaw store. He runs around town chopping off people's heads with the newest power tools. I think you'd like it. It's called 'Conscious Desires.' What are you reading?

I'm reading a very interesting Speculative Fiction book called 'The Passion.' You should totally check it out. It's about a guy that gets buried alive and ends up chewing on a corpse to survive. It reminds me of that Viscerally Gothic novel about the family that lived in the sewers for so long they mutated into werewolves. You know the one... 'Irresistible Amour.'

That's nice, dear. Sounds very literary.

Yuck.

I'm a horror man. I always have been, I suspect I always will be.

That being said, I did notice that the stories in this anthology didn't exactly fall under the same category. Some were slanted one way while some were slanted another.

I considered pulling some of them from the book and putting together a different type of collection, one with an unfailing direction. I decided against it. The range of stories inside this book sits well with me.

A writer compiling a collection of stories is, in many ways, like a musician assembling an album. Sometimes the music on the album will have a consistent flow, and each track will touch the listener in a similar manner. Sometimes an album will take the listener on a journey; each song will be distinctly different than the one before it. Either way, there is no right or wrong. There is only the art form, the artist, and those that appreciate what has been offered. In the end, the artist puts together a collection that feels right. Everything past that is fodder for public scrutiny.

This collection is an excursion rooted in horror. It will take you, literate horror fan, along more than a few unexpected paths. Hope you enjoy the journey. Lord knows you're in for an unconventional ride.

HORROR

THE EXHIBITION

Scott and Penny Beach stood in line for a long time before they were admitted into the exhibition. And while they waited they couldn't help wondering if the show would be worth the bother. Penny didn't think so. She didn't think anything was worth a wait of longer than fifteen minutes. She suggested to Scott—not once, but several times—to forfeit their spot in line, toss the two hundred dollar tickets into the trash, and head to the nearest bar for cocktails, her treat. Each time she suggested this, Scott only smiled.

Normally he would have gone for it; Scott hated waiting in line as much as she did, but he didn't want to miss the exhibition or throw away money needlessly. It wasn't in his nature.

The exhibition was called *The Horror Show*, and Scott was a horror enthusiast. He had books, DVDs, posters, video games, and autographs. To say he was excited would be an understatement; he had never seen a horror *exhibition* before.

The front door opened, the line inched ahead two spots and Penny dragged a finger through her hair, saying, "I forgot to ask... what are the reviews like? They any good? Is it gross... is it creepy?"

"There are no reviews," Scott said with a smug expression materializing on his face.

"Is this opening night?"

"Not really."

"Okay Scott, I'll bite. Why are there no reviews?"

Scott nodded and grinned. "This is a one night only event."

"You never told me that."

"I thought I had."

"No. You said it was scary, but you didn't tell me *that*."

Noise from a streetcar disrupted their conversation. The couple watched it move along the avenue. Scott's eyes fell upon a three-story building that was shamefully vandalized. Two men stood near the building's front door. One man—a tall fellow with thick eyebrows—kicked a dead pigeon with an oversized boot as the other man coughed and mumbled. Both were dressed the same: in tattered, unstylish clothing. Shaggy beards and scruffy hair seemed to be the look of the day.

"By the way," Scott said, "thanks for coming."

Penny shrugged. "No problem."

"Yeah, but this isn't the greatest neighborhood in the world. I'm sure you're not used to it, and I know you don't like this type of thing."

"That's not true. I like art shows quite a bit. I just don't like those stupid movies you're always watching. Most of them are terrible."

"It's hard to argue, but I still love them."

"Yeah, I know. But… they're so fake, Scott. They're poorly written and the direction is awful." Penny stopped herself from saying more, which she could easily do. She liked *good* movies. Scott liked shit. His fascination with that type of trash made her doubt his intelligence. Were all men enthralled in such foolish rubbish?

She looked to her shoes—her sixteen-hundred-dollar peach *gala* shoes—the ones she wore to her sister's wedding thirteen months earlier and hadn't put on since. Without meaning to, she let out a sigh, holding her Prada handbag in her arms like a baby.

Scott knew what she was thinking: she was bored and wanted to go home. "You know, Penny," he said. "You're really beautiful tonight. You look extra gorgeous, like a princess."

Penny's eyes lit up like little suns. "Really?"

"Oh yes. You look as lovely today as the day I married you."

The suns eclipsed. "That was only two years ago, jerk."

Scott laughed. "I know, and you still look good!"

Penny punched Scott playfully and kissed him on the mouth. Scott ran his hand down the back of Penny's dress and gave her rump a little squeeze. As Penny pushed him away, the front door opened. Two people stepped inside the exhibition and the door began to close.

Before it did, Penny stepped free of the line and said, "Mister doorman?"

The man at the door hesitated. "Yes?"

"Can't you let *more* than two people in at a time? We've been waiting for an hour!" Penny flashed her dimples and tilted her head.

A curl of hair swooped across her thin eyebrows, bouncing up and down.

The man at the door smiled. Long teeth sat deep within his mouth. He had cheekbones like elbows, and when he spoke there was a rumble in the back of his throat that sounded like someone digging gravel with a shovel. "I'm sorry Miss... two at a time, that's the way we do. It makes for a better show."

Penny's eyebrows lowered. "Oh."

"And for your information," the man said, "I'm *not* a doorman. This is my family's exhibition. My name is Denoté."

Before Penny considered a response Denoté closed the door with a BANG. The people in line, who had quieted down and listened to the exchange, began talking once again.

Scott said, "Well... now we know. Two at a time."

After a while Penny opened a pack of cigarettes and lit a smoke. The guy waiting in front of them bummed one and shared it with his date. He was an older man with long hair and a tattoo of an eagle on his neck. The tattoo was well designed and inked with a skilled hand. Penny thought it made the man look dignified, not trashy. It was something she would never have admitted.

The tattooed stranger introduced himself as Gary Somers. In time, he said that he worked in real estate.

Scott laughed. "You don't look like a real estate agent."

"I know." Gary responded proudly. "But I'm a nice guy and pleasant to work with. I get a lot of referrals and repeat business. You'd be surprised. This city is loaded with people that prefer working with an agent they relate with. Most sales guys have no soul; it's like they're manufactured in a real estate factory where sex, drugs, and rock 'n' roll never existed. *Here's your haircut, suitcase and nametag. Don't forget to smile politely.* How can you have faith in someone when you don't trust them?"

Scott nodded. Gary was a little over the top maybe, but he seemed honest and straightforward.

The door opened and two more stepped inside, laughing as they entered. As the door closed, Gary's date—a woman who had introduced herself as Angel—said, "Have you noticed that people go in and nobody comes out?"

Penny dropped her smoke on the sidewalk and crushed it with her shoe. "No, but now that you say that... yeah."

"Why is that?"

"I don't know. Backdoor?"

"I guess."

Time crawled. Penny touched up her makeup in a dark window. More people entered the exhibition in pairs and nobody left through the front door.

Finally it was Gary and Angel's turn to go in.

"See you on the other side," Angel said.

Scott smiled. "Have fun."

Thirteen minutes later the door opened and Denoté led them to a ticket wicket. The lady behind the glass said, "Ticket please." Her name was Page.

The tickets were big and gaudy and said THE HORROR SHOW – ONE NIGHT ONLY in giant bold letters. Below the letters, a mediocre drawing of an evil looking skull looked semi-daunting. In the bottom corner of each ticket was the price: $200.00, tax included.

Scott handed both tickets over.

Page said, "Names?"

"Scott and Penny Beach."

Page typed the names into a computer.

Scott and Penny were led to a door. Above it was a security camera.

Before Denoté opened the door, he said, "Mind your step. The art isn't merely on the walls. It's on the floor and ceiling too. It's in the air, the atmosphere. It's everywhere; it's alive. There's only one exit, located at the far end of the building. This show is a one-way street. You can't leave through the front door unless you do it now. You won't have a chance to revisit the exhibitions once you pass them, so enjoy the art while you can. I hope you're not faint of heart. This exhibition is hardcore, designed to scare you to death."

"Sounds good," Scott said. He noticed a smudge of blood on Denoté's shirt; it looked like a handprint. Scott figured it was part of the show. "Looking forward to it."

"Thank you," Penny replied. Her voice was hardly a whisper.

Scare you to death. She didn't like the sound of *that*.

As Denoté opened a second door, Penny wondered why she had allowed Scott to bring her to such a place. This wasn't a gala, this wasn't the theater, this was… well… she didn't know what this was, but it wasn't for her. She knew that much.

Scott and Penny stepped inside the next room. It was small: twelve feet by twelve feet. There was a single light hanging from a black ceiling. The walls were black; the floor had black tiles. On the far side of the room was a white door. There was no art inside the room, no furniture either. It was just an empty room that seemed very dark. The corners were only shadow.

One corner was hiding something: a small camera.

The door behind them closed; they heard the CLICK of the lock.

Penny turned around, startled. She grabbed the doorknob and twisted it. The door wouldn't open. She knocked on the door with her knuckles hard enough to make them red; then she slapped the door with her palm.

Scott placed a hand on her shoulder. "Babe, what are you doing?"

"I don't like this," she said flatly. "I don't like being locked in."

"Why not?"

"It—" Penny stopped talking and looked Scott in the eye. She was going to say *it frightened her*. But wasn't that the point, to be frightened?

"Are you scared?"

Penny laughed in spite of herself. "Yeah, I guess I am."

"Should I remind you that—"

"I know," Penny interrupted. "That's the whole idea, to be scared. But I expected paintings and sculptures, not to be taken prisoner."

"Prisoner! We're not prisoners!"

"They didn't answer the door."

"*He* didn't," Scott corrected. "It's just one guy."

"What about the ticket lady?"

"What about her?"

Penny wrapped her arms around Scott's body and kissed his cheek. "Just don't try any funny stuff, mister," she said. "I mean it. This *stupid* event is going to freak me out enough without you shouting 'BOO' in my ear."

"I won't."

"Promise?"

"Penny, I love you. And at two hundred bucks a pop, I shouldn't *have* to shout 'BOO' in your ear."

"That's true."

"Actually, you know what I heard? I heard that tickets for this thing were going for ten thousand."

"Really?"

"Yeah, and we paid two hundred."

"Not just us," Penny said. "I heard other people in line saying the same thing. Two hundred bucks."

"Huh."

After considering Scott's words Penny said, "Ten grand is bullshit, babe. Either someone lied or they were talking about a different show.

Scott nodded. "I guess. Ready to move on?"

Penny looked at the room. "Is this it?"

"Looks that way."

"Well… this is dumb."

Scott made a face that suggested she was right. "There goes two hundred dollars."

"Each," Penny said with a smile, but she didn't care.

Her folks were rich.

∞∞∞ ☉ ∞∞∞

Lawrence Whitely and his wife Elizabeth sat in the back of the car, listening to Mozart. When the car stopped the driver turned off the music, stepped out, opened the back door, and held out his gloved hand gracefully. The driver's name was Nathaniel Lewis; he was dressed in a pristine black suit and had been driving for Mr. and Mrs. Whitley for eleven years.

Elizabeth took Nat's hand and was assisted onto the carpeted sidewalk. "Thank you," she said, shuffling from the car.

"I'm fine, Nathaniel," Lawrence interjected. "No need to help. This old coupé is still running smooth, thank you very much."

"No problem sir," Nathaniel said, tipping his hat with his fingers. He wasn't surprised; Lawrence never wanted help, even when he needed it.

Lawrence grinned. "I'll call you around ten-thirty, maybe eleven. You can pick us up then."

"Very good sir."

Lawrence and Elizabeth walked up the carpet. A young man in a burgundy suit opened a door. A man in a black tuxedo asked if he could be of assistance. His nametag said Donnie Polanski.

"We're here for the Horror Show," Lawrence said.

"Ah… very good, sir. The party is being held in the President's Conference Suite. Right this way."

Don Polanski led Mr. and Mrs. Whitely through luxurious hallways. When they arrived at their destination Lawrence handed the man a fifty-dollar tip.

"Thank you sir," Don said, and he tucked the fifty into his breast pocket just as neat as he pleased. "Have a good evening."

Inside the room, a man in a grey suit approached. "Good evening sir. Good evening my lady. Here for the show?"

"Why, yes."

"Excellent. May I see your tickets please?"

Lawrence reached into his coat pocket and pulled out two tickets. They were small and elegant, with stylish gold letters written in script. There was no photograph on the tickets, but in the bottom left hand corner it said: $10,000.00 – one night only, limited to twenty tickets.

"Very good," the man said with a brown-toothed grin. "A car is waiting."

∞∞⊙∞∞

Scott and Penny Beach stepped inside the next room, the door closed behind them. They heard the CLICK of the lock, and with that the music began—though 'music' may have been the wrong word. It was a note, a low and hauntingly steady note; the type often heard in horror movies when things turned tense.

Scott smiled; he liked it.

Penny didn't.

The room was twice the size of the first. Like the other room, it was painted black with a single light hanging from the ceiling.

On the left side of the room, three photographs had been pinned to the wall. Each photograph, taken with a Polaroid, was placed five feet away from the next. Above each photograph a small reading light illuminated the image.

They approached the first picture.

It was the image of a dog, a large brown rottweiler. Looked strong.

Penny took Scott's hand, squeezed it, and together they approached the second photograph. This was the image of a table saw, the kind commonly used in a wood shop.

"I don't get it," Penny said.

"Me neither."

They approached the third photograph, slowly, almost cautiously. There was a feeling growing between them that the couple didn't want to address. They were becoming nervous, and not in a good way. They expected art, not this. Not cheap photographs and canned music. This was dark and disturbing, true, but there was nothing artistic about it—at least, not from what they had seen so far.

As they reached the third Polaroid, Penny turned away.

It was the image of a body, a corpse, mutilated beyond comprehension. The stomach was gutted, the chest was mangled; entrails washed the floor around it. A hand had been chewed off; the throat was opened to the bone. Glossy eyes were forever frozen in a gaze of terror.

It took Scott a few seconds to recognize the corpse as a woman, and a few more to see the rottweiler in the background.

"That's fucked up," Scott said.

Penny glanced at the image a second time, saying, "Do you think it's real?"

In the far corner of the room, near the door they had entered, a wall began sliding up. It made a sound like an escalator. They heard a deep, sharp bark, followed by two more. There was nothing *canned* about it.

There was a dog in the room with them, a rottweiler. It ran towards the couple quickly. Its snout was arched into a brutal snarl, with teeth long and white. Its ears were pulled so far back they looked aerodynamic.

Penny stepped away, lost her balance and fell. Her dress yanked against her shoulders; her purse slipped from her fingers and slid across the floor.

Scott watched his wife drop.

His mouth was agape; his eyes were wide with terror.

Looking away from her, he saw the animal leap and he screamed. With his hands held in a distressing pose of defense, he thought he was about to be torn to pieces.

Miraculously—as if God himself intervened—the dog came to an abrupt halt in mid-air.

It was chained to the wall.

"Jesus Christ!" Scott cursed as the animal was hurled to the ground.

The dog lifted itself to its feet, yelping. The hair on its back pointed north. White foamy drool hung from its mouth like a beard.

"What the fuck is that!"

Penny was shaking; she was close to tears. "Help me up," she said. "Scott, give me a hand."

Scott helped his wife to her feet, still cursing and angry. "This isn't art! This is bullshit! Are you okay, honey? Are you all right?"

Penny wrapped her arms around her husband. Her dress—her beautiful peach colored dress—was torn on one side. "Look at me," she said.

The dog growled and barked several times, drowning her words.

"I'm not happy about this," Scott said. "This is bullshit."

"I know it is. Lets get out of here."

As the dog barked again, Scott screamed, "SHUT UP!" He was furious now. That fucking dog was *not* cool.

Hand in hand, Scott and Penny walked towards the white door, eager to move on. The floor was sticky. The white door had spots of blood on it.

They entered the next room; the door closed behind them with the familiar CLICK. This time, the sound pissed Scott off. He tried opening it. Sure as shit, it was locked. Not that it mattered—they *couldn't* go the other way. Not with that fucking dog in the room.

The new room was bigger than the one before it, but designed similar: black ceiling, black walls, black floor, white door and spooky music. But this time, four pieces of art hung from the wall on their left, placed inside three-foot glass cube cases. The art seemed to be 'actual art', not photographs.

Scott said, "Wait here."

He took a step away from Penny and away from the cases, wanting to investigate the dark corners of the room.

Grabbing his arm, Penny said, "Are you crazy? Don't leave me here! You're going to trip some invisible wire and a gorilla will jump out and tear my friggin head off!"

Scott felt the urge to pull away from Penny and tell her to shut up.

He didn't.

"You're right," he said, feeling terrible. This wasn't her fault; it was his. He was the one that brought them here, not her. "I'm sorry. I'm just a little upset about that last room."

"That's okay, but don't leave me."

"I won't."

They walked away from the art, checking out the dark corners. There was nothing to see: no secret doors or hidden panels, no levers or tripwires. Having found nothing waiting in the darkness, they approached the first piece of art.

In the top right-hand corner of the glass cube was another Polaroid print, labeled FIFTY-ONE – MARTIN McCAMMON. It was the photograph of a twenty-year-old man. He had dark skin and dark eyes; he was not looking at the camera. In fact, he didn't seem to realize that he was being photographed.

Beneath the photo, a corpse was humped together in a pond on blood; it looked like the same person. The legs were cut off, the arms were off; each limb looked like it had been sliced a thousand times. In the center of the kid's face, a deep cut traveled from chin to forehead.

The glass was smudged red, like someone had opened the lid and dropped the corpse inside.

The case must be airtight, Scott thought. *Otherwise the blood would be dripping out of it.*

They walked across the sticky floor. Inside the next case they found another photograph. This one was labeled THIRTEEN – CHRISTINE S. HUSTON. It was the image of a woman. On camera she looked pretty. Inside the case she looked like ground beef.

If Scott had to guess, he'd say someone had taken a chainsaw to her.

Inside the third case they found comparable art. The photograph was labeled EIGHTY-NINE – OWEN GLENN. A teenager had been ripped apart.

"God," Scott said, amazed. "These look real, don't they?"

"What if they are real?"

"Yeah right."

"No, think about it," Penny said, completely serious. "What if this is real? That doesn't look like a special effect to me. That looks like a dead body."

"You've seen a lot of dead bodies, have you?"

"That's not the point. Look at it! It's real!"

"Why would anyone do that to a person, and then display it? You're being stupid."

"No I'm not. They'd do it for the money."

"Money? What money?"

"The two hundred dollars."

"They only sold a hundred tickets, babe. That's all that they put on sale. What's two hundred times a hundred?"

"It's twenty grand."

"Twenty? Really?"

"Yeah."

"Still… twenty grand isn't enough money to kill for."

"No? This is a 'one night only' event. Think about it. They set up shop, rent this shit-hole for next to nothing, kill a couple bums, take our money and hit the road."

"I think you're being insane. I also think the people putting on this event were hoping to draw this type of reaction, and with you, it's clearly working."

"Don't talk to me that way."

"What way? I don't want to fight, babe. But think about what you're saying! So this is what, a snuff show? I bought tickets in advance! It's promoted in the newspaper!"

"So what? They could take the money and run, couldn't they?"

Frustrated, Scott put a hand to his head. This sucked. First, the dog scares the shit out of them—and not in a good way—and now this. He wished he had stayed home. "I suppose."

"I'm ready to leave, Scott. I'm tired. I want it to be over."

"Me too."

They walked to the fourth display. It was different than the first three. It still had a photograph (without a number), and it still had a body, but this time the art was a dog. It looked like the same dog that tried to eat them, only mutilated.

∞∞∞⊙∞∞∞

Lawrence and Elizabeth were led from the conference room, down a hall and through a set of doors. There were several black limousines waiting. They sat inside the nearest one and the car began moving. Fifteen minutes later they arrived in a part of the city that neither Lawrence nor Elizabeth had been to before. The buildings were condemned. Derelicts loitered on the street.

"My," Lawrence said. "There sure are making an effort to capture the mood, aren't they?"

Elizabeth huffed. "This is dreadful. I can't imagine what encouraged you to buy tickets for such an event."

"Variety is the spice that makes life worth living, my dear."

"Well, I could do without this."

The driver opened their door but didn't offer a hand.

Mr. and Mrs. Whitely pulled themselves from the car and were led into an alleyway. Elizabeth wondered if they would be mugged. They reached a door. The driver knocked three times, paused, and knocked again. The door opened, and Denoté led the couple up a flight of stairs. The stairs looked terrible. They hadn't been renovated in fifty years.

Lawrence opened his mouth but decided not to say anything. His blooming questions would be answered soon enough, he figured. There was no point in inquiring about the location.

They entered a room that *had* been renovated, walking past two very large, very ugly, men. They looked like escaped convicts that were forced to wear suits. One man was missing a handful of teeth. The other had a scar that ran from his eye to his chin, and a tattoo of a swastika on each temple.

The walls of the room were freshly decorated; pot-lights had been installed in the ceiling. There were elegant paintings on the walls, most of them from the 1800s. There were freshly cut flowers sitting inside stylish vases. There was a fully stocked bar and a man in a tuxedo handing out cocktails. There was a piano with a highly talented musician. His fingers rolled across the keys effortlessly; light jazz comforted the room. The piano sat upon a circle of coffee colored carpet. Where the carpet ended, the room had been remodeled with dark hardwood floors. Stainless steel baseboards circled the space. And on the far side, several large windows had been installed next to each other. Television monitors were above them. Tables and chairs created a living room type atmosphere.

Mr. and Mrs. Whitely were offered a drink and led to their seats. Lawrence requested bourbon. Elizabeth asked for a glass of red wine.

The man sitting in the chair beside Lawrence introduced himself as Buck Million. He wore an oversized brown suit and cowboy boots made of alligator skin. He said, "You've missed quite a show so far, folks. Yes, sir. Don't know how they do it, but it's fascinating, worth every penny."

Lawrence and Elizabeth smiled at the man and looked through the glass. They saw nothing.

"Not there!" Buck said. "Don't look down there, not yet anyhow. The action is in the monitor right now, sure it is. See? Look at 'em.

They're getting ready to move! You'll know when the action is down there. The lights shine."

"Down there?" Elizabeth asked.

"Yep... down there, and they're putting on quite a show."

Lawrence looked at the monitor. A man and a woman were standing in a dark room; looked like they were arguing. The man lowered his head and reached for the doorknob.

Buck said, "Oh boy, here they come. You're gonna love it!"

Lawrence thought that he recognized the couple, but he wasn't sure. The image was too grainy to distinguish faces.

∞∞∞⊝∞∞∞

Scott stepped through the door with his shoulders raised. The floor creaked. The room was dark. He couldn't see anything. Standing inside the doorway, Penny held the door open. The light from the other room was the only light they had.

"What should we do?" Scott asked, with his voice echoing off the walls.

"Why is it so dark?"

"I don't know."

"I can't see anything!"

"Me neither."

The light in the room behind them flickered, and turned off. Now there was only darkness.

"Close the door," Scott said.

"Honey, I'm scared." Penny squeezed Scott's hand hard enough to let him know that she meant business. "I don't like this."

"Close the door."

"Why? What do you know that I don't?"

"The only thing I know for sure is that I want to get out of here. I was in a funhouse one time, inside a very dark room, like this. The objective was to find the door on the far side, but they were tricky, see? I put my hands on the wall and I circled the room. But the door I was looking for was closed. Touching it did nothing; it felt like the wall. I had to circle the place twice before they opened it. Point is... I think were in a funhouse, babe. We need to find the door on the far side."

"I hate this place."

"Me too. Is the door closed?"

Penny stepped ahead and allowed to door to close. They heard the CLICK. New music came on, which was a lot like the old music, but with a slow and steady pulse: BOOMP. BOOMP. BOOMP.

Scott said, "Let's follow the wall and get the hell out of here."

Penny agreed.

Hand in hand, they followed the wall to the nearest corner. The floor seemed shifty and unstable.

"What's wrong with the floor?" Penny asked. She stubbed her foot on something sharp. "OUCH!"

"What happened?"

"I don't know. I cut my foot on something!"

They turned the corner and walked about ten feet before Scott touched a glass case. He wondered if there was a body inside, but he didn't wonder for long. A light began shining from within the glass, growing steadily brighter.

A corpse was revealed. A photograph was revealed too: SIX – RICHARD GOLDSMITH.

Floor creaking, they moved on.

When they reached the next case the same thing happened: Scott put his hand on the glass and a light began to shine. This time, the art was different. The case had a photograph—but no body.

The photo said: SEVEN-THREE – CURTIS RYAN BERRY.

"Why is it empty?" Penny asked.

"I have no idea."

Scott could see the room now, not much, but a little. It seemed like a gymnasium. After he put his hand to a few more cases, he'd know for sure. He stubbed his toe on something solid, dismissed it, and moved on.

"There is something sharp sticking out of the floor," Penny whined. "I think my foot is bleeding."

"Just keep walking."

Scott touched the next case with a trace of excitement. Each case revealed more of his surrounding, like he was unwrapping a gigantic gift. Unfortunately, this sensation was short lived and replaced with the feeling of imminent horror.

The light inside the case crept on.

Both Scott and Penny recognized the corpse. SIXTY-EIGHT – GARY SOMERS.

It was the real estate agent.

His body was in pieces.

∞∞⊕∞∞

Lawrence took a sip from his tumbler, looked at his wife and shrugged.

"I don't get it," he said. "What's happening?"

Before Elizabeth had a chance to respond Buck Million barged into the conversation. "Of course you don't get it! You're catching this act halfway through the performance. Maybe you guys would be better off waiting for the next round. Go talk to the piano man or something, tell him he's doing a good job."

"Next round?"

"Yeah… next round. Every ten minutes or so they sweep up the mess and start again."

"Do you think we should wait?" Elizabeth asked politely.

Buck looked Elizabeth in the eye. "Naw. This here is the best part, the *main* part. You should shut-up with the questions and enjoy. Hell, it's a magic show, that's what it is. A gosh-darn magic show."

∞∞⊕∞∞

"Scott," Penny said. "That's the man I gave a cigarette to."

"No it isn't," Scott said; his voice was barely a whisper. "It… it only looks like him. It's part of the experience."

"Part of the experience? Look! Look at him! Blood is pouring out of his head! See the tattoo? See his eyes! It's him!"

Scott didn't say anything, couldn't say anything.

He pulled Penny away from Gary's box, grinding his teeth together. His heart was beating faster now; his thoughts were reeling. *What if it* was *the man from outside? Could it be him? Was it at all possible?*

Had they stepped into a snuff film?

Were they about to die?

Scott dragged Penny across the creaky floor and heard a strange sound. He knew that sound. (*Oh God, he knew—but he didn't want to admit it, he didn't even want to think it.*) He slapped his free hand on the next box, wanting to see, needing to see. The light inside the box turned on. The box was empty, with the exception of the photograph. He read the name, not that he needed to: FORTY-FIVE – PENNY BEACH.

"Oh my God," Scott said. "What the hell is this?"

Penny's eyes were bright and alluring above her smiling lips. She was wearing the same dress. Her hair and make-up was a perfect match. Yes, the photo was taken today. There was no denying it.

Scott didn't recall seeing anyone with a camera, but then again, he hadn't been looking. Someone could have snapped one easy enough.

Penny began weeping. "That's me! That's my name!"

"No," Scott whispered, but his eyes spoke the truth.

The box was for her.

Suddenly there was a deep, low, growl. The strange sound, he realized, had not been his overactive imagination. And this time, he could not dismiss it.

They were not alone. There was a dog in the room.

"Oh shit," Penny said.

Then the lights came on—all of them.

They were standing in a warehouse. In the center of the room was a large cage. Inside the cage was a dog. It had teeth like daggers.

But could not attack, *yet*.

The cage was sitting on a riser, three feet from the ground, attached to what seemed like, a pulley system. There was a metal cable linked to the top part of the cage that extended high above the animal.

Florescent lights hung from the rafters. Glass cases were attached to the walls. Must have been a hundred of them. Half the cases were empty, save the photo inside. The others were stuffed with the mutilated dead. On the far wall, maybe twenty-five feet from the floor, several windows overlooked the room.

People watched through the windows with happy, smiling faces.

Looking at the floor, Scott gasped.

Unlike other floors, this one was made of unfinished plywood. And protruding from the wood was hundreds and hundreds of spherical blades. Some of them were fourteen inch in diameter. Some were twelve. A few looked to be sixteen. They reminded Scott of semi-circular shark fins, or teeth, or both.

"Table saws," he whispered, remembering the photograph. Hundreds of saws had been attached beneath the floor. This took time; someone wasn't kidding around.

He stepped back and looked at his wife with a new sense of fear.

"Dear Lord," he said. "You were right. This is a snuff film."

∞∞∞ ⊛ ∞∞∞

Buck Million stood up from his chair and lifted a glass in the air. "That's what I'm talking about," he hollered, slurring his words slightly. "Let the show begin! Yah-hoo!"

Someone else said, "Here, here!"

Standing at the window, Lawrence and Elizabeth gazed into the room with the saws. Lawrence crumpled his face into a ball.

What the hell is this, he wondered, *some kind of game?*

Elizabeth saw a man and a woman acting afraid, fake carcasses lying inside glass cases, and saws—probably made of plastic—sticking through slots in the floor. She didn't bother to look at the actors closely, or to analyze the props. She didn't care for this type of entertainment; it wasn't for her.

She walked away from the excitement and sat in a chair near the pianist. The music he played was beautiful. It reminded her of a simpler time, when family was king and people were unadorned and content.

After a fair-sized drink of wine she opened her purse, deciding it was a good time to phone her daughter.

She hadn't talked with Penny in days.

∞∞∞ ⊖ ∞∞∞

Scott saw the people watching through the large windows. He waved his hands in the air. One man waved back, smiled, and nudged the woman on his left. Scott waved twice more before his eyes returned to the blades in the floor.

There was a moment of silence, followed by the sound of a phone ringing. It was Penny's phone, ringing from inside her purse.

Scott's eyes widened. The concept of getting outside assistance hadn't yet crossed his mind. "Answer it! We need help!"

Penny unbuckled her purse and went for the phone.

A door—snuggled between two glass containers—opened, and Denoté stepped through the doorway, grinning like a wolf. He held a shotgun in his hands.

Penny pulled her phone free. "Hello?"

"Hi Penny," Elizabeth said, watching the pianist. She sat her glass of wine on a table. "How are things?"

"Mom?"

Before Penny had a chance to say anything else, Denoté pointed to the far wall and shouted, "That's your exit!"

Scott looked at the exit, and at the saws blocking the path. He screamed, "What the hell are you doing to us?"

Denoté only laughed. "Start the saws!"

As if obeying his command, the saws came to life. The sound was gigantic; it was all Scott could hear. With the saws, the dog began barking hysterically and the music was turned louder to make things more powerful, more surreal. But how much stronger could things get? Wasn't this intense enough?

Penny shouted into the phone: "Mom? Mom? Can you hear me? Is that you? Oh God, I need help!"

She looked at the floor.

The blades were placed in odd angles, giving her room to walk but not much room for error. One missed step and you'd lose a toe, or maybe a heel.

In-between the blades—blood, meat and bones sat in little piles.

Denoté smiled. This was his favorite part of the show. He loved watching people scream. And although many victims ran into the saws like they wanted to get it over with, most just stood there, too scared to move, afraid of the foreseeable future.

Seeing the woman's phone, Denoté decided to accelerate the event. The people upstairs might not like it as much but so what? They had enough entertainment to satisfy the sickest elite minds.

He reached into his pocket and clicked a button on a small devise. The dog's cage began lifting towards the ceiling, setting the dog free.

Once it was able, the animal leapt from its cage, oblivious to the danger on the floor.

Scott saw it coming and screamed in fear.

Penny didn't see the dog until its blood splashed her in the face.

As the animal bounced across several saws, she carelessly stepped away from the carnage. A 14-inch blade ripped her left foot—and her peach gala shoe—in half.

The pain was immeasurable, beyond calculation. Falling backwards, she dropped her phone and screamed. Before she hit the floor her fingers stabbed her face and her hands squeezed tight. A second blade caught her in the elbow, severing the arm. A third blade hit the small of her back. Blood sprayed nine feet in the air. She was pulled across this blade, losing bits and pieces as she moved.

Her eyes rolled back and her mouth fell open.

The people upstairs applauded.

∞∞∞⦿∞∞∞

As Elizabeth listened to her daughter screaming, the people in the room began putting their hands together. Within the clapping and the laughter she heard Lawrence shriek.

"Oh my GOD!" He said with a huff, once he was able to string some words together. He clutched his chest, thinking a heart attack would be unavoidable. He wondered if he was dreaming. "That's Penny down there! And that's Scott! What the hell is this?"

Elizabeth came running towards him, pushing away whoever was in her path. She squeezed herself between Lawrence and Buck and looked into the room.

"Where? Where are they?"

The two men that were standing near the door saw what was happening. The man with the smashed teeth grinned. His name was Russell. "Looks like we've got a situation, Chez."

The disfigured man agreed. "Looks that way."

Chez flicked a switch on the wall and reached into his jacket pocket. A moment later both men were releasing the safeties on their guns.

∞∞∞⦿∞∞∞

A red light began flashing. Scott didn't look at it. He was too busy watching Penny being dragged from saw-blade to saw-blade.

Denoté *did* look at the flashing red light, and he knew what it meant. There was a situation, and it was time to bring this show to an immediate end.

He lifted the shotgun up, and aimed it at Scott.

Scott noticed; it was time to move.

He began running like an athlete, successfully dodging blades for the first twelve feet. Then the shotgun blasted, his toes clipped the jagged edge of a spinning saw blade, and he went down—arms wide, head back, screaming.

∞∞∞⦿∞∞∞

Chez and Russell eliminated people systematically. Russell shot the bartender first, putting a bullet in his head. The man fell back holding a bottle of Sherry. Russ shot the waiter and the piano-man next. The waiter flipped over a chair and the pianist smashed his face against the keys on his way to the floor.

Those mangled notes would be the last he'd ever play.

Chez shot the couple standing closest to him, hitting each of them in the face. They fell like dominoes, one slamming into the other. Then Chez killed whoever seemed easiest, and at this point— they were *all* easy. Nobody was moving yet. Nobody was running. Everybody was standing in a terror pose with their eyes lit up and their hands in the air, saying things like, *"DON'T SHOOT!"* And *"GOOD LORD MAN, WHAT'S GOING ON HERE?"*

The time for fun was now.

One man fell onto his knees begging. He was shot in the heart. Another man wet his pants. He was shot in the balls. There was a woman that looked about sixty-years-old. She had white hair and a dress that went all the way to her feet. Putting her hands in the air, she proclaimed: "I surrender!"

Chez laughed at the woman and shot her once in each tit.

Lawrence put his arms around Elizabeth as if trying to protect her. He felt a pair of bullets entering his back. Elizabeth took one in the eye. They fell to the ground together, lumped in a contorted ball.

When Denoté entered the room he didn't look upset or agitated. He was a professional. This was the business he was in. Sometimes the exhibition went smoothly; sometimes it didn't. Either way—they got paid and traveled to another country.

He walked from body to body, shooting indiscriminately.

And while Denoté and his two brothers finished their dirty work, Page stepped outside and told those waiting in line the bad news. "There was an accident," she said. "Someone has been hurt. The show is cancelled."

When the question of refunds came about she lied, saying a full refund would be issued between three pm and eight pm the following day. Some complained. Some didn't. And none realized how close they had come to certain death.

THE CONFESSION

George was stripped of his belongings and placed inside one of the small padded room inside the police station, which looked nothing like the interrogation rooms he had seen on television. The room was bright and small, six feet by six feet. There were no dark corners creating a gloomy atmosphere, no light bulb hanging from a cable in the ceiling; the room didn't have the famous mirrored window that George thought was commonplace. There was no table to pound an angry fist against and no chairs to kick over in disgust. It was just a box, really—a white padded box with two white padded benches on opposing sides. The room's only door had no knob, only a small murky window you couldn't see through. There was a security camera behind a bubble in a corner, where the ceiling and the wall collided. The floor was covered in cheap brown linoleum. Both padded benches had stains of blood that were hard to notice, and even harder to ignore once they were seen.

George waited for an hour and ten minutes. Sometimes he would sit, sometimes he would stand; sometimes he walked from bench to bench thinking about what had happened. He was sitting with his elbows pressuring his legs and his face planted into his hands when the door opened. Two officers entered the room and took the opposing bench, introducing themselves as Detective Martin and Lieutenant McKean. Neither man was dressed in a uniform. They had white collars and nametags. Martin had a potbelly and short black hair. McKean looked like an Irish boxer in training. His fists seemed bigger than his head.

Both officers offered a hand; George had no choice but to shake them.

"Before we get started," McKean said, "I'd like to inform you that today's conversation will be kept on file." He pulled a small recording device from his pocket and turned it on. Tape started rolling.

No digital recordings here, George thought. He correctly assumed that tape was favored because it was harder to manipulate.

McKean said, "We record everything for continuity reasons, and to ensure the protection of both parties. We'd like to remind you that anything you say can, and will be, used against you in a court of law. You have the right to remain silent, which means you don't have to answer our questions. I'd prefer it if you did, of course. It makes things a whole lot easier on my end, but the choice is yours. Do you understand what I'm telling you?"

"Yes," George said. His voice sounded steady.

"Good."

"Are you okay? Can I get you something, a glass of water maybe?"

"Sure. Water would be great."

McKean knocked on the little window located in the center of the door. The door opened and McKean stepped out of the cell, returning a few seconds later with a small paper cup filled with lukewarm water. He handed the cup to George, and said, "For the record, can you tell us what your name is?"

"My name is George Lewis."

"Address?"

George took a sip of water. "765 Batter Avenue, Oshawa, Ontario."

"How old are you Mr. Lewis?"

"I'm thirty-three."

"Do you have a job?"

"Yes, I work at the harbor, the docks."

"Oh yeah? What do you do there?"

"I load trucks."

"Were you working today?"

"Yes, but just in the morning. I had the afternoon off."

Very nonchalantly, Martin nodded and said, "What time did your shift start?"

George smirked, realizing only then that McKean had begun digging for information. *So this is how the big boys roll*, he thought. *They interrogate you soft and gentle like, so you don't know they're doing it.* This was a shocking revelation. It was so different than the cops he had seen on television that he wondered why anyone would have scripted anything different.

George smiled. "Do I get to make a phone call? In the movies people are always getting one call and using it to phone their lawyers."

Martin lifted an eyebrow. "Do you have a lawyer?"

George leaned his back against the padded wall and ran his fingers through his hair, thinking about his brother-in-law Dan.

Dan was a lawyer; worked in real estate mostly. He was also a big mouth know-it-all that had a part-time gig as an asshole. The idea of getting Dan involved made George feel sick.

"No," he said, admittedly.

"That's what I thought," Martin said. "Believe it or not, most people don't have a law firm on speed-dial. If you need to make a call or two for some reason, just let us know. We're not unreasonable. We're trying to help you here, Mr. Lewis. Understand? Do you need to make a phone call?"

"Not really, I suppose... but maybe later."

"Okay. Let us know and we'll work something out. No problem."

"Thanks. Can I have a cigarette?"

"Sorry. No smoking allowed."

"Come on, please?"

"Sorry."

George pursed his lips together. Of course smoking was forbidden; it was a government building for crying out loud. He said, "I understand that smoking is a no-no, honest. But I'd like a cigarette anyhow, okay? You want to know why? Because I'm going to make things really easy for you guys. I'll give you a full confession if you give me a smoke. Sound like a deal?"

"A full confession?" Martin said. "Do you have something to confess, Mr. Lewis?"

"My cigarette?"

"Smoking is *not* allowed. We don't make the rules, Mr. Lewis. We just follow them."

"Fine. Have it your way."

"My way is that you cooperate, so we can get this ugliness behind us."

George shrugged. "Whatever."

McKean waited a few seconds, then he hit a button on the recorder. A little red light turned dark and the tape stopped rolling.

He said, "Off the record... let me tell you something, George. I'm telling you this, not so you'll feel threatened, or in jeopardy, but so you'll understand. By law we can keep you here for a long while, George. If we have reason to believe that you're dangerous, or thinking about becoming a fugitive, we can keep you here for a very, *very*, long time. But if you're smart, which I think you are, you can be out of here really soon. Helpful people tend to get along better than others, get it?"

He switched the recorder on.

Martin said, "Can you tell us what time you left home today, Mr. Lewis?"

George looked at the floor. He was done talking.

McKean, slightly swaying from character, said, "Should I remind you that we have thirty-two witnesses?"

"Unless I can have a smoke to help calm my nerves, you're going to need thirty-two witnesses."

After a bout of silence, Detective Martin stood up and knocked on the window. The door opened and Martin disappeared. A moment later he returned with a cigarette, an ashtray, and a book of matches.

He placed the items on the padded bench and said, "I'm not giving you a cigarette, Mr. Lewis. However, you're a grown man and you're old enough to make your own decisions."

"Thank you."

McKean looked annoyed. He didn't enjoy bending the rules, not even a little. It made him feel like a bad cop. "Are you going to talk to us?"

"You bet." George took the cigarette, leaving behind the matches and the ashtray. "I was coming into Toronto from Oshawa," he said, tucking the cigarette behind his ear. "I was alone. I got on the six fifty five. Like usual, a thousand people got off the train and nobody got on. The train, as you might know, brings commuters from Toronto to Oshawa in the evening time, and it returns to Toronto near empty."

"Of course," Detective Martin said. "Rush hour... everybody's going home."

"Exactly."

McKean asked, "Why were you going into Toronto on a Tuesday night?"

"I met a girl a few weeks ago."

"Name?"

"Kelly something. She's a real cutie. We hit it off and swapped digits and I wanted to see her again. My wife and I are divorced... well... separated. We've been apart for more than a year. If it wasn't for my little boy I'd probably never see her again." George looked at his knees. His eyes stayed there for the longest time. His shoulders were slumped and his hands were clasped together, almost prayer like.

"You were alone?"

No response.

"Mr. Lewis? On the train, you were alone?"

In time, George said, "I was alone, sitting near a window. My car was empty and I didn't have anything to read. There were a few newspapers lying around, like always, but I read most of them at work. I didn't have much to do... except look out the window. It's a nice trip most days. The train runs along Lake Ontario and the sun shines off the water. During the summertime you can see the girls sunbathing. Well, it took about ten minutes for the train to get rolling. And I'm sitting there, not thinking about much. Just looking out the window and watching the buildings roll by." George swallowed uneasily. His fingers tightened and the muscles beneath his shirt bulged. His eyes drifted; he was a man lost in thought. "Then I saw the strangest thing."

The room grew quiet and stayed that way.

Detective Martin began feeling uneasy. "Well, Mr. Lewis...? Don't keep us waiting, now. What did you see?"

George looked up, almost startled by the voice.

"A man," he said with a solemn tone. "At least I thought it was a man. I don't now. He was standing in a field, close to the tracks. He was alone, wearing a suit and a tie. Black suit, black tie, white shirt. He had a little crown of white hair wrapped around his head and his face was all wrinkled. His eyes were gray but they were brilliant, too. Just brilliant. They were so bright they seemed to be sparkling." George almost laughed. "Now... I'm in a train, remember. I'm moving fast. So for me to notice his eyes..." George trailed off.

McKean cleared his throat, and said, "Is the man doing something that catches your attention?"

"Not yet."

McKean nods. "Okay."

Martin said, "How old do you think he is, roughly?"

George looked up and grinned. "A hundred and fifty."

Martin's eyes widened with shock. "A hundred and fifty years old?"

"Yeah, he was at least that. He was older than any man I'd ever seen. I'd tell you he was two hundred but you'd think I'd lost my mind." George put a hand to his mouth and nibbled on his nail. "I didn't think much of the guy at first," he said, talking through his fingers. "Why would I, right? Yeah, well, after five minutes or so the train stopped. A couple people got aboard and sat near the door."

"What did they look like?"

"Who, the people that got on? They were nobody, just teenagers. Two boys: sixteen, maybe seventeen. They kept to themselves. They don't matter. Trust me, they weren't a part of this."

Martin nodded his head, trying to understand. He didn't like the sound of that last sentence: *They weren't a part of this.* For some reason that sounded bad to him. It sat in the air like dialog from a bad movie.

A part of this—

What the hell did that mean, anyway?

George cleared his throat. "We started rolling again. After a few minutes I'm looking out the window, watching the world roll by, and I see him again."

"Who did you see?" Martin asked, his voice, slightly uneasy.

McKean glanced at his partner oddly, but said nothing.

"The old man in the black suit, of course. Who do you think? He's standing at the shoreline, right near the water. And he's looking at the train, watching us go."

McKean, holding back a grin, used a voice that was best suited for small children. "Am I missing something here?

"Nope."

"It was the same man?"

"Yep."

"And the train was moving."

"That's what I said."

"You know that's impossible, right Mr. Lewis?"

"Yeah. It's impossible, all right. I know. And that's exactly what I tell myself. I tell myself that it's impossible, that it's not the same guy. That it has to be someone different. And at a hundred miles an hour I make myself believe it. I'm no fool, and I'm not getting a good look at this guy. Within seconds he's in and out of my line of vision, so it has to be someone different, right? Some other two-hundred-year-old-man standing near the tracks in a black suit...

"Well the train stops. I guess we're at the Ajax station now. The two kids by the door get off; nobody gets on. I'm alone again. We start rolling and I'm looking out the window, you know? I'm watching. Part of me is hoping to see him again because... well... because it's interesting. Another part of me—the part that's getting worried––is praying that I don't see anything. I know the odds are slim, but I don't want imaginary friends standing at the edge of the tracks. I don't want to live in the nuthouse."

McKean shifted his recorder from one hand to the other.

Martin kept his eyes glued on the suspect.

"Sure enough, the train gets rolling and I've got my face up to the window. I'm actually leaning my head on the glass at this point. I don't care. I want to see what's out there and I don't want to miss him—if he's there, which, of course, he's not going to be... right? *Wrong*. After a few minutes I see him again. Same black suit, same black tie, same white shirt. He's standing next to one of those old buildings with the graffiti on it. To be honest with you, I can't believe it... I really can't believe it. But it's him, all right. Three times I see him. But at this point I'm still thinking it has to be three separate people because it *can't* be the same guy, it just *can't* be. I'm in a train, for crying out loud. There's no way it can be the same man and I know it. Well, I watch him for as long as I can, trying to burn his image into my head just in case I see him again. But can you imagine? Jesus rode a bicycle... can you imagine seeing the old guy a *forth* time? He'd have to be a ghost, wouldn't he?

"Well, we're moving at a good speed, not as fast as before but we're zipping along... and I can still see him. He's getting farther away all the time but he's still there, standing by the tracks, and do you know what happens? Can you guess? He *waves* at me. The son-of-a-bitch waves, as if to say, '*Yeah George! It's me! You see me and I see you, now what are you going to do about it?*' Well I don't mind telling you that I got scared. Right then and there—for the first time in years, I got scared. His eyes were glistening and his hand was swinging back and forth and he had a smile that looked more like a scream than anything else, like he was wearing the goddamn thing wrong, somehow. So why wouldn't I be afraid? Huh? I don't mind saying, I damn near dropped a bucket of shit in my pants."

The two officers didn't speak, nor did they exchange a glance. They just listened, nodding their heads like good cops do. There would be time for talking later, plenty of time.

George let a few seconds roll by, waiting for a response that didn't come. Then he said, "The train stops again. This time a dozen people got on board. I'm not looking at any of them. Oh no, I'm looking out the window. The train starts moving. It went under a bridge and along two or three subdivisions and sure enough, I see him again. Four times, now—*four!* Only this time we're not racing along the track at a hundred miles an hour, we're going slow, like… twenty miles an hour, slow. And he's looking at me. And his eyes *are* sparkling, like he has little flames inside his eyelids. His eyes are huge and gray and sparkling and I *know* they're focused on me! I know it. And the man's not alone. Oh no. Not this time. This time he has a little boy with him. The boy is five or six. The old man has a hand wrapped around the kid's wrist and he's holding him up so his feet aren't quite touching the ground. The kid's arm is extended in a way that looks terrible, it has to be hurting him, and, and…"

George squeezed his eyes together and pulled the smoke from behind his ear. He lifted the matches, lit the cigarette, and inhaled the nicotine. It helped. Didn't fix anything but it helped.

Detective Martin said, "What about the boy?"

"I don't remember what he was wearing, if that's what you're asking me, but I remember the pain in his face. He was hurting, all right. He was in a lot of pain. The old man had a hunting knife in his free hand. It was long, like a machete. He had the boy in one hand and the knife in the other. The boy was screaming. His eyes looked like they were trying to jump out of his head and he was screaming like a baby. Now, at this point I'm thinking: *What the hell am I going to do?* I want to get off the train and help the kid out somehow, but every time I see the old man he's halfway between stations. I'm not even sure which way I should go, 'cause I know I'm going to see him again, and I know I just passed him.

"The train stops and I think about jumping off, but I don't do it. I don't know why. More people climb aboard, the car is getting full now… now that we're close to Toronto. We start moving and five minutes later I see the old man a fifth time. The boy is there, lying at the old man's feet with his throat slashed open. There's a huge pool of blood around him, like every ounce of fluid has been drained from his body. And the old man is laughing. He loves it, I can tell.

He's laughing and smiling and he loves it. And that's not the worst part. The worst of it is, the old man has another kid with him. This time it's a little girl, and she's screaming, just like the boy. He's holding her up by her pigtail; her feet must be three inches from the ground. I don't know how he did it. The girl was small but she must have been heavy, too heavy to hold up like that. But he's doing it. Somehow the old man is doing it. Her feet are kicking and her hands are grabbing at his wrists. The old man is waving his knife in the air. He's laughing and showing me who will die next, see? I get it, but what the hell should I do, huh? Can you tell me that? Should I call 911 and tell them I LOST MY FUCKING MIND?"

"Sir," Detective Martin said, startled by the outburst. "Maybe you should calm down. Have a drink of water."

George took another drag.

McKean bummed the smoke and snatched a drag too.

"The train kept rolling. We stop again. We start again. I'm not looking out the window now. I've had enough. I figure it's me, you know? I tell myself that it's just my imagination, but it's not and I know it. After a while I look out the window. I have to. I can't help it. And as soon as I look out I see him. The boy is at his feet and the girl is next to him. Both children are lying dead in a pool of blood that's so big it looks like the pair has gone swimming, and he's laughing, and smiling, and holding up another child. He's holding up *my son*. MY SON!!!"

"Sir—"

"MY SON WILL BE THE NEXT TO DIE! GET IT? DO YOU *GET IT?* AND HE'S *JUST A BOY!*"

"Sir you need to calm down." McKean said, wondering if there was going to be a problem. He hoped not. He tried to avoid every problem he encountered.

"FINE," George said, loudly. His eyes were the image of pain. "Now I'm *LOSING* it—and I don't know what to do! I'm praying... *praying* I've gone insane, you know? And maybe I have, but I don't think so. And I make a decision: I'm getting off the train and going back. I'm going to get my son because I *can't* sit on the train any longer. I don't want to see what happens next. I don't! I can't take it!"

"But then something happened," McKean said. "Didn't it?"

"Yeah. Something happened all right. I see them: three dead children, lying in a pile. My son David is near the tracks with his arms and legs bent out of shape. He looks like a broken swastika. His eyes are wide open and his throat is cut from ear to ear. My heart dies right there in my chest. I looked over my shoulder and I see the old man. He's sitting right next to me, inside the train! His eyes are sparkling and he's smiling like a lunatic. He says, '*Did ya see something interesting there, George? Did ya? Did ya see somethin'?*' And that's it. I jump up from my seat and I start choking him. I choke him so hard that my knuckles turn white and my fingers get sore. And the whole train is screaming now, screaming at me! They're trying to pull me off and some crazy bitch is laughing like a witch and I'm not letting up, because I know. I *know!*"

George took another drag. McKean stole a drag too.

"It doesn't occur to me until later that this thing isn't human. How can it be? It has to be something else, get it? It has to be something from a different world!"

McKean nodded, thinking the guy was a nut-job. He had seen his fair share of them. They came in all shapes and sizes.

"Do you really think that, Mr. Lewis?" Martin said, almost mockingly. "Do you really think that you saw somebody from another planet?"

George ignored the question, lost in his own storytelling. "I saw the sparkle fade out of the old man's eyes and I knew that he was gone. I knew it was over. Then somebody kicked me and somebody else dragged me outside. I didn't try to fight them. I killed the bastard that murdered my boy and that was good enough for me."

"You killed a forty six year old man," McKean said. "A high school history teacher."

George wondered if they had been listening. "But it was him... it was the old man."

"No," Martin said. "It was a man named Dean Peavey. He had a wife. He had children."

"Oh no! This guy's eyes were sparkling, like he had little firecrackers inside of them or something. It was the old man. Trust me."

Detective Martin looked at his partner. He said, "Do you mind giving us a moment, Lieutenant?"

McKean nodded, stood up, and knocked on the window. The door opened and the officer left the room.

For a few seconds there was silence.

Then George, with his eyes facing the floor, said, "I don't care if you don't believe me. My boy is dead. I have more important things to think about."

Martin grinned.

"Oh, I believe you, George. I believe you. But you strangled the wrong guy. I wasn't inside the schoolteacher when you killed him. I moved on. I was inside that crazy bitch you heard, having a good laugh."

Martin put a wrinkled hand on George's lap and smiled. And when George looked up he saw that the cop had aged a thousand years. His eyes were glistening. Worst of all, his smile was all wrong.

He had a smile that looked like a scream.

MONSTERS

BABY

"Wait!" Jennifer said, somewhat urgently. She was standing in the doorway with a white coffee mug in her hand, looking excited and worried and absolutely beautiful. The cute little hearts on her silk pajamas were shiny and red, complementing the cherry polish on her fingers and toes. Her dark hair was cut boldly short. If her face wasn't so stunningly gorgeous the cut may have looked terrible because she had a boy's haircut, really. It was brave and it worked, but somehow it seemed best suited for a nine-year-old brat with ice-cream stains on his t-shirt and the knees knocked out of his blue jeans.

Richard, standing on the driveway next to his car, turned towards his wife. Complementing his bright green eyes and his slender nose was a smile that seemed more dimple than lip. With a smirk, he said, "What is it?"

"Just come here for a minute."

"But—" Richard had a travel bag in his left hand and his car keys in his right. He lifted them up and flaunted them, as if doing so was a statement onto itself.

"I know, honey," Jennifer said, using her 'baby-needs-some-loving' voice. "I know, but I have to tell you something. It's important."

Richard unloaded a hearty laugh. "Now? You need to tell me something important, now? The clock is ticking and I've got to go! Steve is probably wondering where I am already."

"Please, hon. I thought it could wait but now I don't think it can." She tilted her head to one side, scrunched up her expression and stood on her tippy-toes. Coffee splashed inside the mug.

Richard placed his luggage on the driveway and dragged his feet towards his wife. With his shoulders slumped, his eyes sad, and his face long, he looked like he was visiting his mother on death row. Should have been a stage actor. "What is it?"

Jennifer wrapped her arms around his waist and kissed him on the lips. Once the kiss was planted she nuzzled into him, and said, "I love you."

Richard laughed. "Well that's fantastic. I love you, too."

"No, I want you to *really* hear me. I love you, Richard Beach. I love you with all my heart. You're the best thing that ever happened to me, and I'm unconditionally yours."

"Aww…" Richard felt his belly flip as an unexpected batch of tears threatened to break free from their hiding place. She had said that very thing on their wedding day; it was part of her vows. Hearing it again was wonderful, and—*my Lord*, he treasured this woman. She was everything he wanted and more. She was artistic and beautiful; she knew how to make him feel like the luckiest man alive. Every hour they spent together seemed better than the one before it. And sure, his friends might argue that they were still in that honeymoon stage; they might even point out that things were bound to change, but still—if Jennifer wasn't the perfect woman he wasn't sure such a thing existed. With his eyebrows raised and his arms around her, he granted her a soft and loving squeeze. "You're so sweet."

"Tell me that you love me."

A smile blossomed. "I love you."

"No… really *tell* me. Make me understand."

Richard kissed his wife with as much passion as he could muster. He ran one hand along the center of her back while caressing her neck with the other. He whispered, "I love you Jennifer Samantha Beach. I love you more than you'll ever know. I'd die for you in a heartbeat, because you are the very best part of me. You are my everything; my center; my one. I'm so lucky to have you in my life, Jenn. I know it and I'll never forget it. I love you, baby-doll. I love you; I love you; I love you." He kissed her again.

Exploiting his emotions felt liberating and fabulous. He wanted the moment to last forever. It didn't. Jennifer pulled away while their lips were connected. She took him by the hand and looked him in the eye.

All business, she said, "I'm pregnant."

Richard flinched. "What?"

"You heard me. I'm pregnant and I want to keep the baby." Her eyes stayed with his, and when he tried to look away she gave his arm a yank. "How do you feel about that?"

Feeling manipulated, which wasn't a feeling his wife evoked very often, Richard allowed a moment of undisciplined honesty. "Shocked."

"That's a far cry from being overwhelmed with joy."

"Yeah, but..." A fumbling of words led to: "I thought the doctor said you'd never have children? What happened to that?"

Jennifer huffed, offended. "This is good news, right? You love me more than I'll ever know, correct?"

"I'm just—"

"You're not happy."

"I'm surprised, is all... of course I'm happy."

"You don't look happy. You don't *sound* happy either."

Richard turned towards his car, ignoring the fact that his wife was perturbed. He needed get behind the wheel and drive, because continuing this conversation was dangerous and disturbing and an assessment of his thoughts wasn't going to help anything. He *wasn't* happy; that was the truth of the matter. He wasn't the slightest bit pleased. If anything, he felt scared. And maybe a little sick.

He said, "I've got to get going."

"Just like that? You're leaving me?"

Richard swallowed back whatever emotions were bubbling to the surface. He could feel a cold shiver sashaying up his spine as his stomach churned into concrete. "Look," he said, faking a smile. "I'm happy. This is great. We're going to start a family and I think that's excellent, but I have to go... Steve's waiting. Let's talk about it later."

Jennifer's eyes morphed into slits. She wasn't thrilled but she didn't want to fight. "Will you call me?"

"I'll try, but you know how work gets. If I don't get a chance to call you tonight I'll see you in three days."

"Are you mad?"

"Mad?" Richard smiled, and this time he didn't fake it. "I'm not mad. This is great news, honey... really. Like I said, I'm just surprised. I thought we were going to adopt." He kissed her then. It was uncomfortable and clunky and the opposite of affectionate. And although he wanted to restate the fact that he loved her, somehow he couldn't find the words.

He turned away with a sigh, made for the car, and tossed his travel bag into the trunk. After he jumped behind the wheel he gave his wife a little nod and hit the road. Lips pursed, dimples lost, he didn't look back. He didn't even wave. Five minutes later he parked against the curb so he could cry his eyes out without driving into a tree.

∞∞⊛∞∞

They'd been sitting next to each other for thirty-five long minutes and Steven Wendelle knew damn-well that something was bothering Richard from the moment he sat down in the car. He could see it in Richard's eyes and hear in his voice, which wasn't exactly non-stop with discussion. The pain appeared to be rooted directly into the lines of his face, chewing at him like a virus, turning him into an old man before his time. But Steven was a good friend, his *best* friend, and sometimes a best friend must bite his tongue. He figured this was one of those times. Besides, the conversation would happen sooner or later. It always did, once Richard was ready. He wasn't the type of guy to bottle things up forever.

Thirty-five minutes became forty-five. Forty-five became an hour and fifteen. The grace period was over; it was time to put dinner on the table.

"Okay," Steve said. "Spill it."

"What's that?" Richard's voice was little more than a croak.

"I'm not blind, you know. I'm not stupid either. Clearly, something's wrong. Tell me what's bothering you, otherwise the rest of our journey is gonna be painful."

Richard took a moment, not because he didn't want to talk with his friend but because he needed a moment to put his thoughts into words. Finally he settled on, "It's Jenn."

"I figured. You guys fighting?"

"I wish it were so simple. No, we're not fighting. In fact, we've been getting along wonderfully."

Steven's face turned grave. He tapped a hand against his leg, saying, "She's sick." It wasn't a question.

"No, that's not it."

"No?"

"No. She's not sick, she's… oh, this stinks."

"What is it?"

Fingers tightened around the steering wheel. "She's pregnant."

"What?"

"You heard me. She's *pregnant.*"

"Oh shit."

"I know."

"I thought you said she couldn't get pregnant?"

"That's what the doctor told us. Twice."

Steve looked absolutely stunned. Time rolled by. Finally the question was asked, the one Richard had been asking himself all morning. "What are you going to do about it?"

"I don't know."

"Are you going to tell her?"

A deep breath. "I don't think I can. It'll ruin everything."

"You can't let her have the baby, you know. Don't even think it."

"Oh, I know. Letting the pregnancy continue isn't an option, but she won't have an abortion. I can't even ask."

"Are you sure?"

"Yes, I'm sure. An abortion is out of the question."

"If not that, what? What's left?"

"Well, to be honest, I was thinking of poisoning her. I'd be careful not to kill her, of course. But a high dose of those-morning after pills might, well... you know. Maybe I could crush them up and slip 'em into her food for a week or two."

"Will that work?"

Richard's voice suggested it was a long shot, when he said, "Honestly, I can't really say. I think you're supposed to take them the next day, after sex. I don't know... I don't know what to do, Steve. I'm lost."

They drove for another hour, stopped for lunch, and continued on. Conversation was minimal and for the most part, light-hearted. At one point Steve offered, "If there's anything I can do, just ask." But there was nothing he could do, nothing obvious anyhow, and both men knew it.

Day became evening.

They drove along a forgotten highway that few cars traveled. Cedar trees to the left of them, cedar trees to the right. A large hawk flew overhead as they turned onto a dirt road that led to a pathway that could hardly be deemed a trail. Deep in the woods, they were. Lost with the black bears and the insects, the crows and the deer. Lost in a place they called their own. Steve had purchased the land years earlier. *Picked it up for a song,* he said. *The money he paid his lawyer to square the deal was equal to value of the land,* he said. Steven Wendelle was no bullshit artist, and Richard knew he spoke the truth. Twenty acres of nothing—it was absolutely perfect.

As the sun began setting and the moon began to rise, they stripped down to their underwear and placed their clothing in the car. Sitting on a log, hands in their laps, they waited. Quietly. Peacefully. The August air was warm. It was fresh. The fact that Richard lied about working for the weekend wasn't relevant. He loved his wife and she loved him. He also loved the sounds of the forest, which were comforting and serene. All thoughts concerning Jennifer and the seed in her belly was set aside. Other things were swiftly becoming more significant.

Richard was the first to feel the change coming on. He felt it in his spine and in his teeth. His knees popped and his shoulders buckled. Then, as he watched his hands grow long and his fingers turn to claws, he tried to articulate how much he enjoyed the transformation. What escaped his throat could only be described as a growl. Animal thoughts consumed him. A thirst for blood boiled inside his brain.

Steve didn't notice these things happening to Richard; he was too busy becoming a monster.

The hunt would soon begin.

∞∞∞✷∞∞∞

On the third day, right around the time Jennifer was expecting her husband to arrive home from his monthly trip, there was a knock on the door. She looked out the window and was surprised to find a police car in the driveway. She opened the door cautiously, wondering if she had done something wrong.

Two officers stood by the door. Expressions were solemn. The one that spoke first looked young enough to be in high school. He was lanky with eyes that bugged out of his head. The other cop, thirty years his senior, had a chocolate complexion and dark hair.

Jennifer sized them up quickly: the veteran was showing the rookie the ropes; they probably didn't have a thing in common.

"Mrs. Beach?" The rookie said, clasping his fingers together.

"Yes?"

The veteran stepped forward with his chin raised, taking control of the situation. In his hand was an envelope, which he gripped very tightly. "Are you Mrs. *Jennifer* Beach?"

Jenn nodded. "What seems to be the problem?"

The older cop removed his hat and held it near his chest. The rookie followed suit.

"Mrs. Beach, my name is Officer Wright and this is Lieutenant Moscowitz. I'm afraid we have some bad news for you."

Jennifer's eyes danced from man to man. She looked at the hats in their hands and the way they were standing. She looked into eyes brimming with shame. The rookie's shoulders dropped an inch as his stare found the floor. Oh, shit. They were about to say something terrible. They were about to say—

"There's been an accident."

Something inside Jennifer collapsed. Or died. The earth tilted on one corner and the air thinned. As the room began to spin she managed to say, "It's Richard."

"I'm afraid so."

"There's been an accident."

"Right again, Mrs. Beach... on highway 78. I'm sorry to inform you—

(oh please God no)

—that your husband—

(don't say it, for the love of God)

—is no longer with us, Mrs. Beach,—

(I don't want to hear this... please tell me I'm dreaming)

—I'm afraid that he's dead."

A question tumbled from her lips: "What happened?"

"It happened this morning around seven-thirty; a head-on collision. There were no survivors."

A one-sided conversation was laid out like brickwork. Officer Wright explained and described and enlightened and in the end it didn't amount to a hill of beans. Richard was dead, gone forever. Nothing else mattered.

At some point the envelope was placed inside her trembling fingers and the officers offered condolences that came from the heart. A short while later they left her to grieve. Alone. She couldn't be more alone if she tried. And when she closed the door on a world that was eternally altered, she wondered how she'd ever find the strength to face the day.

∞∞⊙∞∞

The next three days were arguably—or perhaps not so arguably—the hardest days of Jennifer's life. She was still a young woman, twenty-nine this past March, and her life had been cruising along rather smoothly. On paper it may not have seemed that way. Her mother died when she was barely eight years old. The death had been hard on her, of course. But that was twenty-one years ago and twenty-one years is a long time for a woman not quite thirty years old. She could remember her mom's face, but mostly from photographs. She could remember her mother's voice, somewhat, and she had the memory of her mom gardening in the backyard. After that it was just little clips and snippets, not full-blown memories, really. More like recollections.

Her father was a different story.

He was an alcoholic she visited twice a year; his name was Ted. He wasn't a terrible man; he never intentionally hurt Jennifer or abused her physically, but he prayed at the altar of intoxication and was very devoted to his religion.

Ted took a bus into town on the day of the funeral and offered what he was able in terms of condolences. But Jennifer could smell the whiskey coming from his mouth and see it in his blood-red eyes. And when he announced that he couldn't stay Jennifer felt a weight lift from her shoulders that was heavier than she realized. She was already dealing with one catastrophe. When she looked into her father's slack-jawed face she felt like she was dealing with another.

It wasn't a perfect life, as no life is. Her mother was dead and her father was—for lack of a better word—gone. But it wasn't a bad life either, and she wasn't an only child. She had a younger sister named Kate who was just as bright and beautiful as she was. And it was Kate that embraced her after the funeral, although the reasons for it were not what Jennifer expected.

∞∞⊙∞∞

It was a day of tears. Richard and Steven were buried in the same cemetery at the same time. A double funeral at noon, two separate wakes shortly after. Jennifer hosted one; Steven Wendelle's parents hosted the other. For Jennifer, the last of her guests didn't leave until almost seven. And when they did, Jennifer and Kate found themselves sitting at the kitchen table, surrounded with food and beverages. The refrigerator had already been filled to capacity; the countertops were equally loaded. Jennifer was grateful for the generosity of her friends and family, but what she was supposed to do with so many provisions was beyond her.

Kate said, "I'd like to stay with you, if that's alright."

Jennifer was drinking rum and coke, unlike Kate who was drinking gin. Alcohol wasn't something they indulged in often due to the negative influence it had on their childhood. But here, now, it was just what the doctor ordered.

Jennifer took a drink, then said, "It's okay. I'll be fine. Honest I will. You should be home with Mike, not here with me."

Mike was Kate's husband. They had been married four years.

Kate, who was looking a little tired, said, "Actually, no. I don't think so. I want to stay here. Do you mind?"

"Why? Is everything alright?"

Eyes fixed on the table, Kate fought against a faltering voice. She tucked a lock of hair behind her ear and said, "I'm not offering charity, I'm asking for a favor." She looked up, expecting her sister to press for details. When it didn't happen she reluctantly explained her situation. "Mike and I are finished. He's been cheating on me, and we've been fighting, and our fights have been getting physical."

Jennifer was shocked. "He's beating you?"

"Not exactly." Kate shrugged. She took a drink. Ice cubes clinked inside the glass, accentuating the silence of the room. "To be honest, we've been beating on each other. He never hit me first, but he hit me a few times after I hit him. And I *have* hit him. *Hard.* And he deserved it. But I can't do this any longer. I can't sit in the house alone, wondering when he's coming home, or *if* he's coming home. I've been following him around at night and he's been... oh, God. It's so bad. Everything is *so* screwed up." Kate swallowed back a sob, before saying, "If Richard was still, well... you know... *alive* (the word came out in a whisper), I wouldn't ask. I'd probably just deal with my problems until Mike kicked me out or moved out himself. But if you're going to be *here* alone, and I'm going to be *there* alone—crying, or fighting with my asshole husband, well..." A tear rolled down her face. "I want to be here with you. I'm asking if I can stay."

Jennifer took Kate by the hand. Nobody would call her selfish at a time like this, but somehow, that's how she felt. She had been so caught up in her own life that she failed to glimpse into her sister's. Kate's world had been falling apart for however long and she didn't even realize it. It was shameful, really. And yes, it *was* selfish. Worst of all, Kate was more than just family; she was Jennifer's truest friend.

Voice miserable, Jennifer said, "Of course you can stay with me. Oh, hon. I'm so sorry."

"I'm sorry too.

"This sucks, doesn't it?"

Kate wiped a tear from her face using the palm of her hand. "It sure does."

They cried and drank and talked for hours. Later they watched *Legally Blonde*. Much like the alcohol, an hour and a half of Elle Woods seemed to be just what the doctor ordered. Kate stayed the night. The next day she went home and packed her bags. And three months later, when Richard showed up at the door, dressed in the suit he was buried in, it was Kate that let him inside.

∞∞∞⊙∞∞∞

Kate was living with Jennifer full time now, and her relationship with Mike was officially over. They talked on the phone. They went out for coffee. They slept together one final night and it was during sex that Kate discovered her love for the man was truly gone. The trust had vanished, the bond was destroyed, and the bed they shared seemed to be carrying some terrible secrets—secrets that would haunt her for as long as she allowed them to. Her future felt like a better place without the damaged remains of her marriage clinging to it like a bad smell. So she asked her 'soon to be ex-husband' not to call, and although there were many nights that he wanted to, he respected her wishes and left her alone.

When the doorbell rang, Kate was cleaning up the kitchen and Jennifer was, unfortunately, in the hospital. She had been having problems with her pregnancy—reoccurring pains were getting worst as time moved on.

The last batch of agony was almost four weeks ago, three and a half weeks into her second trimester. It lasted nearly three days. During that time she found herself buckled over on the floor, screaming at the top of her lungs, one hand clutching her belly, the other tightened into a fist that was pounding on the hardwood like a jackhammer. And although Kate was absolutely furious with her, Jennifer wouldn't visit the doctor until well after the pain had subsided. Kate didn't understand why; she *couldn't* understand why. And Jennifer couldn't explain it. But deep inside she knew something was terribly askew in a way that made her feel nauseous with fright. The child inside her body was scaring the hell of her, not just because of the pain she felt but also because of the atrocious thoughts that had been swirling around inside her head like a cyclone.

Jennifer was having nightmares—*terrible* nightmares on a nightly basis. She kept thinking about *Rosemary's Baby*, not the movie but the book. She had started reading it the day before she told Richard she was pregnant. She finished it forty-five minutes before the policemen gave her the news. Being the type of person that enjoyed Christmas stories in December and spooky stories on Halloween, she thought it'd be fun to read Ira Levin while pregnant. How unfortunate. Now her days were spent wondering if she'd find herself surrounded by doctors and nurses that were chanting "Hail Satan" after she gave birth to a child with a forked tail, little horns, and eyes that belonged to a goat.

When Jennifer finally found the courage to have her herself examined—a full week after she was sprawled out on the floor, kicking, screaming, and drowning in pain—the doctors were seriously concerned. Not just for the welfare of the unborn child but for Jennifer as well. For reasons they couldn't explain Jennifer's uterus had been torn in several places and she was bleeding internally. She also had bruises on her fallopian tubes, a pair of swollen ovaries, and a cracked rib. Needless to say, she was at risk of losing the baby. Worst than that, her life seemed to be in jeopardy as well.

Her stay in the hospital lasted for five days. During that time she had two minor operations. After that, Dr. P. Hollis, the head physician, made her promise that she'd return immediately if the abnormal pain started to flare up again. She agreed.

Earlier in the day the pain returned. And although she was afraid to have the baby examined while the aches were progressing, the fear of the unknown had taken control of the situation. She left for the hospital alone, informing Kate by phone hours after she arrived.

Kate swung the door open without looking through the window. Had she looked, things would have played out differently.

Richard was there, leaning a dislocated shoulder against the wall. He looked bad. Beyond bad. His back was twisted; his neck was broken. The top half of his skull had been crushed like an orange that had been stepped on by a very large foot. Both of his eyes were still in place, but one had turned dark and the other sat deep within its damaged socket. Parts of his brain bulged through a long crack in his face and his bottom lip had been torn free.

Kate stepped back, fingers on her mouth, eyes like baseballs. Her jaw dropped as her heart rate accelerated. She was going to scream—*had* to scream, because screaming was the only logical thing to do.

Surely, this *couldn't* be Richard. It *couldn't* be the man she considered a perfect match for her sister. Not him.

She looked away from his face.

Hanging from his shattered frame was a suit that must have been worn by the Incredible Hulk because it was tattered and frayed in ways that didn't make sense. The pale, dehydrated skin on Richard's hands seemed to belong on a living corpse. More so when he lifted those hands—hands that were covered in a thin layer of dirt, hands that were connected to arms with unnatural looking joints and elbows, hands that were reaching out.

Oh God, he was reaching out.

Kate's mouth was still wide open, but the scream she was looking for was hiding deep inside. Soon she'd find it, and when she did she would set it free. She would—

"Wait," Richard said. He tried to smile but with half his teeth smashed out he looked absolutely ghastly. "Please wait. Don't scream. I'm still alive... so help me, Kate. For the love of God, help me."

"Oh shit," Kate said, staggering back another foot. Her hand remained on her mouth; her bottom lip began to quiver. "What the hell is this?"

"I'm not dead... I was *never* dead." Richard dragged his left foot forward. His balance was reassigned and his right foot followed. The movement alone looked painful. "Help me come inside."

Just like that, Kate started crying. She couldn't help it. Her body was shaking and her knees trembled and full-sized tears were running down her cheeks. Had she not just used the bathroom she may have suffered an accident. To say Richard's presence was making her nervous would be like saying a pitchfork in the face might leave a mark.

She babbled, "But... but..."

"Help me Kate, I mean it." Richard slumped into the house and tossed a broken arm around his sister-in-law.

Kate screamed then. It slipped out before she knew it would happen. She screamed long and loud and when she was finished she screeched, "Oh, I'm sorry. Oh Richard, I'm *so* sorry. What do you want me to do?"

"Help me get to bed... and I need some water."

Despite the way he looked, and despite the fact that he smelled worse than death, Kate helped Richard into the bedroom and assisted him onto the bed. Doing so made her skin crawl, but what else could she do? Running away was possible, but this was *Richard*. He was family *and* friend. And most of all, he was in dire need of help. Besides, the notion of running came with an unsettling side-thought: *what if he chased her? What would happen then?*

Once Richard was settled Kate turned away, planning to fetch the water. Mostly she just wanted to be somewhere else, away from him, away from the monster.

Richard grabbed her by the arm. "Where's Jennifer?"

Still terrified, Kate said, "At the hospital. I was on my way to see her." This wasn't entirely true but in another thirty minutes it would've been.

"Why?"

"She's having complications with her pregnancy."

Richard mumbled, "I bet she is." Then he looked out the window, sizing up the darkening sky. "Do you know what time is it?"

"Seven-thirty? Maybe eight?"

Richard groaned. "Listen, Kate. Listen to my words and hear me well. Don't tell anyone I'm here. Don't call the doctors; don't phone the police. Don't explain things to your husband and don't go yapping to your father. It's got to be our little secret, Kate. You understand me? Nobody can know I'm back."

"But why?!" Kate's emotions were getting pulled in every direction now. She felt like laughing and screaming and yanking the hair from her head in bunches. "You need help, Richard! You need medical attention right away!"

"No!"

"Are you serious?! Look at you, Richard! You look like—" She was going to say that he looked like a goddamn stiff but instead she asked: "What happened? I was at the funeral, you know... I was there!"

Richard coughed. Greenish-brown pus-like drool dribbled along the place his bottom lip should have been. He said, "Me too. I was inside the box, Kate. Inside that fucking coffin, unable to move, unable to scream." Richard paused. His thoughts twisted this way and that. Suddenly he wanted to explain everything. He wanted to tell her that he was alive when they scraped him off the road, and when they brought him into the morgue and embalmed him. He wanted her to know that he was alive when they boxed him up and covered him in dirt. He wanted her to understand what type of man he *really* was, and that he couldn't be killed in traditional ways. There was so much he wanted to say, so much he needed to explain. Choosing his words carefully, he said, "They thought I was dead, and I might have *looked* dead, but a car accident can't kill me. Not ever. And in time I get better. I *always* get better."

Kate couldn't believe what she was hearing. It was impossible. It was *insane*. But she knew what she was *seeing*, and what she was seeing had to be some type of sick joke. She asked, "How can this be happening?"

"Doesn't matter. What happened to Steven?"

"Who?"

"Steve, the—"

Kate realized what Richard was asking. She said, "Oh. He died in the accident." As an after-thought, she added, "With you."

Richard's thoughts turned a corner. He wondered if Steven was still trapped in his coffin, scratching the silk, trying to get out. He pushed the thoughts aside and said, "You've got to call Jennifer... tell her to come home right away. Can you do that for me?"

"Of course, I'll call her right now. But Richard, what in God's name should I tell her?"

"Tell her to come home. If she wants to know why, say I need to talk with her. It's very important."

∞∞∞⊙∞∞∞

When Jennifer hung up the phone her face had become pale. *Richard was back. He was alive. He wanted her to come home. It was important.*

She couldn't believe it.

Alone in her hospital room, she pulled herself from bed and dressed quickly. She ran her fingers through hair that no longer looked stylishly brave, but messy and without a hint of fashion sense. She made for the exit with her shoes untied, her skirt on sideways, and her travel bag hanging wide open. A car-ride later she shuffled through the front door of her home, sun setting in the west, moon rising in the east, clutching her belly with her fingers.

The child was kicking; the pain was getting worse. If it didn't soon subside she was going to find herself buckled over on the floor, screaming bloody murder. Again.

As she staggered down the hallway towards (her late husband) Richard, the bedroom door blasted open and Kate stepped into view. Her eyes were entirely different now. They looked swollen and red, like she had been screwing her fists into her sockets for the last five years.

She grabbed Jennifer by the shoulders and said, "You need to brace yourself."

"Let me see him."

"No! Listen to me Jenn; you need to prepare for what you're about to see. Richard is back, but he looks bad. He looks *really* fucking bad."

Jennifer cringed. She hadn't heard her sister use the F word since she was fourteen years old. She said, "I'll be alright."

"Brace yourself! I'm not kidding about this."

Jennifer pushed Kate away forcefully and plowed into the room. She figured she'd be able to handle it. No problem. She was a grown woman, for crying out loud. Besides, how bad could it be?

Richard was on the bed. His body was angled unnaturally and his suit was covered in dirt. Chunks of brain were resting on the pillow. A large bug ran across the sheets as another scurried up the wall. To summarize, he looked like an embalmed corpse that had been smashed to pieces with a sledgehammer and pulled from the earth he'd been buried in. And Jennifer, truth be told, didn't brace herself for what she was about to see; she didn't brace for anything.

"Oh my God!" she shrieked, with eyes growing wide. "Richard, is that you?"

Looking like a zombie, he said, "Listen to me, baby-doll. This is critical."

The thing living inside Jennifer kicked.

She staggered, clutching her belly.

At the same moment, Richard felt his spine expand. He said, "You need to kill the baby inside you. You need to do it right now. Get a clothes hanger; push it in. Abort the child."

Kate stepped into the room, quite literally trembling and pulling at her hair. She said, "What are you talking about... abort the child? *Now?!* What the hell is happening here?!"

Richard's knees popped and his shoulders buckled. His teeth elongated as his fingers turned to claws. "Hurry!" he managed. "Before it's too late!"

Eyes on her husband, Jennifer groaned. She could feel something chewing her apart. Then her knees faltered and she dropped to the floor. Pressing her back against the nearest wall, her body convulsed. Not once, but three times quickly.

"My baby," she whimpered.

She ripped open her blouse; buttons popped in different directions. Looking at her stomach, and seeing the strange way the child was moving beneath her skin, she almost understood. *Almost.* Then when she looked at Richard an important piece of the puzzle clicked into position. It felt like a hard slap in the face, and it was horrifying. She had a monster living inside her, a goddamn monster, trying to get out—Richard's child.

And Richard was—

Gone.

In his place was something most people will never see: half man, half wolf, bones mending, muscles growing, nose becoming snout, arms becoming legs, hair morphing into fur, hands turning into paws, eyes still green, still the windows to the soul of a man that's able to comprehend the situation. But his mouth was growing larger and more dangerous with each passing moment. Teeth seemed to be everywhere. Jaws opened far too wide and words escaped like hostages. They were hard to recognize, but much harder to ignore:

"Abort. The child."

Kate, standing in the center of the room with her hands in the air, looked away from Richard in horror. She saw Jennifer leaning against the wall with her blouse pulled open and her skirt hiked up. Her knees were shaking and her pink underwear had turned red. She had one hand cradling her belly as blood leaked from a long tear in her skin, through her trembling fingers, over her wedding ring (a ring she couldn't bring herself to remove), and across her unpainted nails. She said, "Please Kate, Richard's right. Get a clothes hanger. Help me abort the child."

Kate watched her sister endure two quick spasms before a mist of blood sprayed from her mouth. It ran a line down her chin and dripped onto an exposed breast. There was blood between her legs, a dark red puddle. It was growing larger. Kate didn't understand what was happening and she didn't understand why, but she knew one thing for sure: her sister was dying, being ripped apart from the inside.

Yes. They had to abort the child.

She looked across the room and her eyes locked on the closet door. In no time at all the door was open and she was standing in the doorway, pushing bags out of the way with her left hand while pulling shirts off hangers with her right. But there was a problem: all the hangers were made with plastic. She couldn't see any of the old-fashion metal kind. She grabbed a jacket and a vest and threw them to the ground in a pile.

Jennifer screamed.

Richard growled.

And Kate, cursing under her breath, saw what she was looking for: a rusty old hanger, nastier than a snake. She snagged it from the rack and stepped towards her sister, trying desperately to keep her eyes away from the huge thing that was laying on the bed, covered in fur, snapping its jaws, eying her like a fresh meal after a long day.

She said, "We need to get out of here!"

"No," Jennifer whispered. "Just hurry, Kate. Hurry!"

There was no time to argue so Kate bent the hanger this way and that, playing it like an accordion, trying to snap it. She didn't think she'd be able to unravel it fast enough, and time was so important now. Oh yes it was. She thought about running for the second time that evening, but Jennifer was in no position to follow her lead, and she couldn't leave her sister behind.

Richard growled, sounding like a grizzly bear.

Jennifer screamed again. And Kate screamed too, frustrated with the time she was spending. Her hands were working as fast as they could but it wasn't fast enough. She didn't think the hanger would ever break but suddenly it did. It broke right where she wanted. It almost seemed like a miracle.

Straightening the wire, she turned it into a long, narrow spear. Then she dropped to the floor, positioning herself between her sister's legs.

Jennifer's eyes widened. She looked desperate now—desperate and in serious pain. She lifted her knees, stretched her legs apart, and grabbed a hold of her blood-soaked underwear. She pulled the dripping cloth to one side, exposing her vagina. Gasping and begging, she said, "Do it, Kate. Kill it. *Kill* it!"

Kate caught a frightful glimpse of her sister's belly before pushing her labia apart with her fingers and plunging the wire in. But one glimpse of Jennifer's stomach getting ripped open was enough: skin splitting, muscles tearing, blood pouring to the floor in generous amounts. There was a coil of flesh that appeared to be growing and when Kate saw it her stomach clenched and she thought she might pass out. It was too late to perform a back-alley abortion. It *had* to be too late.

Looking Jennifer in the eye, Kate forced the wire deep inside.

And Jennifer, gasping her final breaths, writhing in agony, looked up. Not at Kate. Oh no. There was a monster in the room now, standing high above, gazing down at the girls with its terrible green eyes, teeth like daggers, bloodlust boiling inside its brain.

Richard was gone.

And although Jennifer knew that her husband had become something entirely different—something bred without love or affection—memory of the man she married seeped into her heart and she managed to say, "I love you with all my heart, Richard Beach. You're the best thing that ever happened to me. I'm unconditionally yours."

A GHOST IN MY ROOM

Last night I saw a ghost in my room, the ghost of my wife Luisa. I was lying in bed when it happened. The light was on—not the bright one, just the little one that sits on the table beside the bed. One moment I was rehashing my day and reading a magazine and the next moment she was there. I didn't notice her at first; I didn't see her appear. But I felt that something was different, something had changed. So I looked up, not expecting to see anything out of the ordinary, and there she was, looking in my direction.

Her skin was pale and wrinkled, her dress was sopping wet. She had long runners of seaweed tangled within her hair, which for the most part was clinging to her face and skull. Her nose had begun to rot around her nostrils. Her eyes were glossy; her white orbs and the skin around them was so incredibly dark and dreary that I wasn't sure it was her—but it was. Oh God, of course it was her. A man knows his own wife when he sees her, even when she looks so bad.

I sat up quickly, placing my weight on my elbows and resting my back on the headboard. Then I pulled my knees towards my chest and away from her, careful not to make a sound as I did so. I briefly considered jumping up from the bed and running for the door, but my fear had me paralyzed. I wasn't going anywhere.

Besides, is it possible to run from a ghost?

Somehow I doubted it.

She was in the far corner, hiding in the darkest place, where the wallpaper peeled from the wall. I hated that empty corner. Somehow it always seemed like the coldest spot in the house.

Try as I might, I couldn't pull my eyes away from her face—her terrible, terrible face. She looked like she'd been underwater for a year or more. Her lips were blue and her teeth were black with soot.

I could smell the ocean salt on her body, polluting the air around me. She was all craggy and... sour. That's what she was: sour. She smelled like a river. Lord above, help me; my wife smelled like a truckload of rotten fish. And she didn't move, not a goddamn muscle. She didn't breathe either. For the longest time she just stood there, looking at me with white-button eyes while tiny crabs scurried across her skin. Doing nothing, saying nothing, like I should say something to her! And I could hear the drops of water falling from her dress. They hit the floor one at a time, slowly, almost keeping rhythm.

Drip, drip. *Drip*. Drip, drip. *Drip*.

It was the only sound in the room; the only sound I could hear. It creeped me out immensely. The minor splashes against the hardwood made things all too real.

Drip, drip. *Drip*.

She opened her purse.

Yes, she had a purse. It was covered in patches of green and brown moss. Strange huh? A dead woman with a purse... wonders never cease.

She opened her purse, slid her bony fingers inside and pulled something free. Her fingernails were dirty, cracked and broken; the bright red paint had washed away long ago. Her knuckles looked to be nothing more than lumps of bone. Her feet started moving slowly, one after another, making squishing sounds on the floor. She was coming towards me, dragging her feet and holding a wet plane ticket where I could see it. When she reached the bed a crab fell from her open mouth and onto the sheets. It scuttled over my knees and onto the floor. Then another crab fell, and another. Each crab was smaller than a coin. Just babies, really. Just babies.

I wondered if there was a nest somewhere on her body.

With a gurgle in her voice, the ghost said: *"You won't let me go, will you? Tell me you'll keep me safe."* Her lungs were filled with seawater, which dribbled from her chin.

I opened my mouth but I didn't say a word. My lips started to quiver and my knees began to shake.

"Tell me."

"No," I said. The word seemed to pop out of my mouth on its own. "I won't let you go."

"Promise me?"

"Of course," I said, almost babbling. "I promise not to let you go, honest I do. I promise I'll keep you safe."

She put the ticket in my hand. One of the crabs started running towards me and I screamed; I couldn't help it. The ticket was cold and wet and I just couldn't take it. I screamed loud and squeezed my eyes shut and held my fists against my ears. The ticket crumpled into the shape of my hand and knowing it was still there I screamed again.

When I opened my eyes Luisa was holding me in her arms nervously, saying, "What's wrong, dear? What happened?"

I pulled away from her. I must have looked insane. "I don't want you to go away, babe," I said. "Oh please, don't go! Don't leave me!"

"But why, honey? Why?"

I looked across the room with my stomach in a knot and my teeth clenched tight.

The ghost was gone. The crumpled plane ticket and the crabs were gone too. The two of us were alone now; the house was empty once again.

Things had returned to normal.

∞∞∞⊙∞∞∞

That was last night.

Today Luisa's plane crashed into the ocean, like I knew it would.

It went down somewhere off the coast of California around 4pm. Two-hundred and fourteen lives are expected to be lost. They're still looking for survivors, but I have no hope twisting in the winds of my imagination. I know in my heart she's lost.

When I heard the news I didn't cry; I didn't say a word. And tonight I'm here, lying alone in my bed for the first time in years. I can't sleep; I can't think straight. I keep waiting for her to visit me again.

I need to apologize; I know I do. I should've tried harder to keep my promise.

I should have tried harder to make her stay home.

JONATHAN Vs THE PERFECT TEN

Jonathan Weakley stood at the edge of the Pit like a proud father, looking down at his latest monstrosity. This time it was a wolf spider. The time before that it was a scorpion. Guessing the spider's weight, he put the number in the ballpark of 750 pounds. The scorpion he presumed to be half that.

Ninety percent of the town came to watch the event, same the time before. But everyone knew today's experience was going to be different, very different.

Scary different.

Some were excited, some nervous, and many had a hard time grasping the realities of what they were about to witness. These people—and there was more than a few of them—were juggling terror and disgust with equal portions of shame and wonder.

The other ten percent—*the missing ten*—were God's People.

God's People were the town's Bible pounding naturalists, easily appalled by Jon's labors. They had been storming Monk Town hall two or three times a week, saying Jon was a wicked sinner, a madman; the devil's henchman.

On the other side of the fence, Jon thought God's People were oppressing technology, the future, science, and everything evolution had to offer. This sightless religion-monger minority didn't offer new ideas or add to society. They just told people what they did wrong, while acting like progression was a sin and inventiveness was against the law.

With the town's population being 730 people, knowing who had your back and who didn't was easy.

Jonathan knew.

He knew who was trying to supersede his genius: God's People.

∞∞∞⊙∞∞∞

Jon charged a flat rate of one dollar a head to patrons, and the fee came with weeklong viewing rights. It was expensive; no one could argue that. But Jonathan knew what he was doing and what hands to grease.

$650.00. That's what came through the door, same as last time and the time before. $650.00 meant six-hundred-and-fifty people paid and seven didn't. The seven included himself, his brother Ted (who sold tickets), Mayor Monk, Sheriff Wellston, Deputy Gorman, Bernie Gorman (who published the Monk Town press), and old Bill Watt who had been hired to work the cages.

That left seventy-three people boycotting the event. Seventy-three in a town of seven-hundred-and-thirty—that was ten percent.

A perfect ten.

It was almost funny.

∞∞∞⊙∞∞∞

One man alone ran Monk Town: August Monk.

August was the mayor and the muscle. He could shake hands in the morning, murder in the afternoon, and kiss babies in the evening. Not to suggest that he was a tyrant. No, that would be misleading.

Mayor Monk was a family man before his wife and son past away. He had kind eyes, a nice smile, and wasn't afraid to laugh. But he kept a mental detachment from his work—his *peacekeeping*—as he liked to call it. He had a simple philosophy: cause trouble in my town and you'll swing from the gallows pole. If you don't like it, live somewhere else.

He didn't care about explanations. Screw around; meet your maker.

The people in town respected August for that.

He thought it was funny what people found admiration in.

Months before Jon's first creature unveiling (the first was a two-hundred-and-ninety pound rat with pink bubble eyes that were the size of a fist and thirty-inch whiskers) Jonathan made a point of having a sit-down with Monk. He shared his thoughts with the man, hoping to gain the town's support.

He said, "Well sir, I'm going to charge fifty cents a head and I expect to pull in sixty townspeople. That's $30.00. Now listen here while I tell you something, and feel free to look me in the eye while I'm tellin'. This shindig is costing a lot more than thirty bucks. Chemicals alone are three times that, food is at two bucks a month now and I've been investing money for years. But I see a future in this zoo of mine, and soon folks will take notice."

Monk did something with his throat that sounded like a wet grunt. He said, "Fifty cents? That's a lot of money, Jon. People in town don't have fifty cents to look at a big rodent. You know that. Where's your head?"

Jon nodded. "I want to agree with you, Monk, I really do. But I've given this more than a little thought. I figure I'll pull in sixty people, maybe sixty-five."

"Sixty-five? Boy, you are dreaming."

"Keller will come."

"That's one man."

"And he'll bring his family."

Monk had a square jaw, beady eyes, and thin lips that came together in a way that made him look tough when he was thinking about money. He looked tough now, looked like he was thinking. "Yeah, maybe."

"Let's say he does. That's him, Ellen, and the five young ones. That makes seven people right there, and you *know* he'll bring the little ones. He'll do it because he can, and he'll do it to show off."

"I suppose."

"He will. And do you think Absonoff will stay home, a big shot like him? Not a chance. He'll be there because of Keller, and he won't be comin' alone neither. And once Absonoff decides to go, old man Macmillan will get the fire under his ass. You know that."

"Yeah."

"And then there's Norton King. He wouldn't miss out on a thing like this, not in a million years. And he can afford it, might not want to shell out the cash but he will. Why? Because he don't skimp on nothing, believe you me. And what do you think Laura will say when Norton decides to go to the zoo without her? Any ideas?"

"Okay, okay. I see your point. Now that I think about it Wendell and Markus wouldn't miss something like this. They'd walk a mile in the rain to see a wet turd."

"Yeah, not to mention 'what's his nuts' up on the hill."

"Gentry."

"That's right. Gentry. He'll come. He'll be first in line."

"Sixty huh?" Monk was looking tougher and tougher. His thin lips puckered into a horizontal button that was threatening to disappear altogether. He was seeing possibilities in Jon's foolish idea, dollar signs too. He grinned, releasing the button that was his mouth. "Do you really think you can bring in sixty? That's a lot of people, Jon. A lot."

"It'll be a 'one week only' event, and whoever buys a ticket can to come all week long if the mood strikes 'em. Yeah, I recon the zoo will bring in sixty. Like I said… might even bring in sixty-five."

Monk rubbed his hands together. "Okay, lets pretend I agree. What's in it for me?"

"Well August, I've given this a fair bit of thought too. I know you're tough, but I believe you to be a man of your word."

"That's why I'm running the show."

"Exactly. Now look-it, I could give you this or that, but I want you to help me nurture the damn thing. We'll get sixty this time and seventy or seventy-five next; who knows? Might get eighty. You know this town. There's nothing to do but sit around Bunter's Saloon, gettin drunk and talking shit. And by the way, what do you think they'll be yappin' about after the zoo opens, huh? The zoo, that's what… they'll be talking 'bout the zoo. My zoo. Your zoo. *Our* zoo. You get me?"

Monk's little lips began to pucker again. "Uh-huh."

"Hell, if someone farts loud enough half the town comes runnin' to see whose shorts got dirty."

"It's hard to argue there. That new game, what is it called?"

"Bingo."

"Yeah, *bingo*. It's more popular than I thought possible… picking numbers to win a basket of tomatoes? I don't get it."

"That's 'cause people are bored, August. There's nothing to do here."

August Monk grunted. Jonathan Weakley was telling the unbiased truth about Monk Town: it was a boring place to live. He didn't like it much but it was the truth.

"Now listen," Jon said. "I want to give you twenty-five percent. I'll cover the cost of food and the growth enhancing chemicals and the rest of it, don't worry 'bout that, but what I'm tryin' to say is: I need your help. I need you to give me Town Pit and wave the three-dollar fee. And talk the zoo up, tell people they shouldn't miss it... that sort of thing."

"What's that work out to, six bucks? Is that right?"

"Help me out and before long, your cut will be twenty dollars."

August squeezed his lips together. He didn't think he'd see twenty, not for a big rat. But he was wrong about bingo so he figured he might be wrong about the big rat too. And the town *was* boring; he had to admit it. He said, "If this zoo idea falls flat you owe me three bucks for the Pit plus my percentage. Sound fair?"

"Sounds fine Monk, just fine."

∞∞∞⊕∞∞∞

That first week they didn't bring in sixty or sixty-five. They brought in a hundred and forty-eight. The admission total was $74.00. Monk's cut was $18.50. He couldn't believe it. It was the easiest money he'd ever made. Stranger than that, Jonathan Weakley was an instant celebrity. Some considered him a hero.

And the people couldn't get over the size of the rat.

It wasn't big; it was huge.

To put it in perspective, a 290-pound rat is the size of a full-grown hog. People thought he captured the damn thing.

And they were thankful—none more so than Helga Whitman.

Helga was the first to call Jon a hero.

She said, "Can you imagine that monster finding you face down in the garden? Good Lord, it'd swallow you whole! Jon is a hero for capturing that abomination, a true hero! He should get a metal!"

It was later—after she discovered that Jonathan was responsible for growing the animal—that she formed God's People.

She hated Jon then, felt like a fool too.

For the first few weeks Jon enjoyed his fame; he never thought people would react the way they did. It made him happy, but it also made him worried. He had the feeling that if people discovered the truth about the rat he might be in hot water.

Monk agreed; he felt it too.

So the two men decided to keep a lid on the science part of Jon's zoo. Problem was, Jonathan's experiments weren't exactly a secret, and in time the information leaked and everybody knew the truth. Fortunately, it was a slow leak, and people didn't seem to care.

Except for the perfect ten, that is. And they cared enough for everybody.

∞∞∞⊙∞∞∞

The second event sold two-hundred-and-two tickets, $101.00 at the door. Monk's cut was $25.50; he couldn't have been happier.

But this time it wasn't a rat; it was an 850-pound lizard.

The lizard looked like a dinosaur and ran around the Pit with so much speed and might that people thought it would jump free and kill them all. It gave one hell of a fine performance. The spectators went home happy and filled with astonishment.

After that, things sort of went into production.

Jonathan hired Bill Watt and his brother Ted to build a permanent cage over the top portion of the Pit so the animals couldn't escape. (After the lizard's little run around the park, escape seemed very possible.) The men also built permanent cages inside the Pit for the rat, the lizard and whatever came next, sparing no expense. After the cages were finished, they started installing seats around The Pit's rim. They were nicely crafted, made of leather. And they weren't costing Monk anything, so he was all for it.

The Pit sat empty most of the year; there were a few dances, the odd wedding, and the annual Monk Town auction. But Bingo was held in *Town Hall* not *Town Pit*, and when it came right down to it—if August rented Town Pit ten times a year (at three dollars a day) he considered himself lucky.

Ten times three equals thirty bucks.

And Jonathan had given $44.00 inside a ten-week span.

So, as far as August was concerned, the Pit was Jonathan's zoo now. The weddings, the auction, and whatever else came down the pipe, could take place at Town Hall—end of discussion.

∞∞∞⊙∞∞∞

The third event was announced fourteen weeks later. It showcased a 330-pound bullfrog; they sold 260 tickets. Six weeks later they showcased an 800-pound turtle and sold another 296 tickets. That was a total of 556 tickets and $278.00 at the gate.

Monk put $69.50 in his pocket.

He figured he'd soon be rich.

Unfortunately the turtle never moved and people went home displeased.

Jon felt that his reputation had taken a beating, his pride too. So he turned things up a notch and mutated something more dangerous: a wolf. By opening night the man-eater was 900 pounds and looked like a water buffalo. Its eyeteeth were four inches long and its snout was the length of your arm. It could easily bite a man in half.

Five hundred and twenty people lined up to see the wolf, nearly double the amount that came for the turtle. People saved for weeks, and Jon raised the admission price to sixty cents. It was a bold move considering the disappointing reviews the turtle received, but in the end the gamble paid off.

520 times 60¢ was $312.00.

Monk's cut was $78.00.

It was right around then that God's People started getting organized.

And Jon came up with his cage-match idea.

∞∞∞ ☉ ∞∞∞

Helga Whitman, the woman who first labeled Jon a hero, was Monk Town's local Bible thumper. She was tall and gangly and her feet looked like snowshoes. Her knuckles were white and somehow bloodless looking; her hands were forever balled into fists. She had a husband named Dale, who had a face like a turnip and tragically bugged-out eyes. He acted like he wore the pants in the family, which, of course, he didn't. But nobody cared one way or the other so nobody disputed it. The pair made a fine couple. He was stupid and she was obnoxious. And for Helga and Dale, the campaign against Jonathan's zoo started at home.

They had three children: Betty, Bailey and Mandy. All of them were girls. All of them were as ugly as the back end of a cow; poor things never had a chance, really. At eight, ten, and eleven years of age, what the hell did they know about right and wrong and the lay of the land? Nothing. Not a goddamn thing.

They were the first to be recruited.

Next on the campaign trail was Walter and Ruth Huppert.

Walter had a face like a hamster and Ruth was so fat she made her own clothing. Everything she wore looked like a sack. The two of them combined weren't bright enough to peel a bag of potatoes...

and they had nine children. The youngest was two and the oldest was sixteen, and of course, the sixteen-year-old had two children of her own. Two boys. That made a total of thirteen people living under one roof.

Recruiting them was easy. Walter and Ruth were dumb enough to climb on a porcupine. And when they signed up, the family signed up too; they had no choice.

Next stop: Father Maloney.

Maloney was a quiet, peaceful man. He was a man of God who thought Jonathan was doing some interesting things at Town Pit. But that didn't change the Church's view of: *no man shall play God*, so when push came to shove, and Helga stuck the petition under his nose (with eighteen signatures, no less) Maloney sided with God's People. He felt that he had no choice.

He also felt like moving to a different town.

War was brewing. It was easy to see.

With the Church in her pocket, Helga and Dale went door-to-door preaching the Lord's word and hunting signatures. Some told them to piss up a rope. One couple laughed and one man tried to start a fistfight with Dale; most folk politely said they didn't get involved in politics. However, there were a few that coughed up a signature, pledged their allegiance to the Lord and said, "I will not support Jonathan Weakley and his satanic rituals."

Those poor unfortunate bastards thought it was the Christian thing to do.

Once Helga and Dale were done gathering signatures something strange happened, something nobody expected.

People choose sides.

Until then, a good chunk of the town didn't care what Jon was doing. They heard stories and though it was interesting, but considering something interesting and pulling your ass off the couch are two different events.

That changed.

Now folks wanted to see what the fuss was about. And three weeks latter, when Jonathan showcased a twenty nine-foot gorilla, the zoo enjoyed its first sell out. The evening was a huge success. The beast was breathtaking; it looked like King Kong. Seven weeks later the zoo had its second sell-out showcasing a 560-pound wasp with clipped wings. A couple months later Jonathan enjoyed his third sell-out, showcasing a 1,900-pound rattlesnake. The forth sellout was a 9,000-pound grizzly bear. Then came the scorpion. Then came the wolf spider.

Helga was pissed. And ready for war.

∞∞⊛∞∞

As time marched on, August Monk grew very tired of God's People. Every few days they came to his office complaining about Jon's zoo and Satan and whatever seemed to be the hot topic of the day. Helga was always there, along with several dimwitted followers, and she loved flashing Monk her list of 73 names.

"They gave me their signature and their hearts to the Lord," she was fond of saying. "The town supports me but most of them are afraid to get involved! That's the only reason they didn't sign!"

Monk found it hard to believe that the very people that were supporting Jon's zoo wanted it shut down. And if they did, tough shit. With Jon constantly raising the admission prices he was making good money; that zoo wasn't going anywhere. And Monk was no fool. Those 73 names were misleading at best. What Helga was really waving around was fourteen idiots and a bunch of children.

He said, "Jon's zoo is a part of Monk Town now, Mrs. Whitman. You might as well get used to it."

But of course, she didn't. This was her cause. She figured an animal would soon break free and there'd be pandemonium in the streets.

Didn't happen though.

What happened was a fistfight at Bunter's Saloon between Helga and Bill Watt, forcing Monk to crawl out of bed and deal with the uproar. And with that, the fate of God's people was decided.

They were to be exterminated.

∞∞⊛∞∞

Jonathan Weakley stood at the edge of the pit like a proud father, looking at his latest monstrosity, the 750-pound wolf spider.

August Monk stood at his side. "You ready, Jon?"

"I'm ready."

"You sure 'bout this? It's not too late to change your mind."

"Oh I know, but I want to get rid of the rat and the bullfrog, and losing a few others won't be the end of the world. I can re-stock the zoo. Besides, this is going to be fun."

"Absolutely." Monk said. He closed his eyes and raised his hand.

On the far side of the Pit, Bill Watt began spinning the handle on a crank-wheel. Down below, a large metal door lifted from a cage. Once the door was completely open, Bill spun a different handle. This caused the back wall inside the open cage to move forward. And as this happened, out came the perfect ten, God's people, all seventy-three of them.

They were in the pit.

And they were terrified.

Six-hundred-and-fifty-seven pairs of eyes looked upon them. Mouths were hanging wide open. And for a moment, nobody said a word.

Then Helga walked away from the others and stood in the center of the dugout with her hands balled into fists. She didn't look afraid; she looked like she was trying to lead her people.

She lifted her chin and said, "Friends and neighbors, look around you. Look at what you're doing and what you have done! This is not the Lord's way. This is Satan's doing, the pathway to hell. The Dark Lord is leading you astray."

Monk didn't want to hear it. He said, "You sure Jon?"

Jon nodded and Monk raised his hand a second time.

Bill Watt took hold of a large handle that was attached to a complex pulley system. He spun the wheel.

Eleven cage doors began opening at once.

The wolf snarled. The gorilla began beating its chest. The rattlesnake hissed and the rat scampered in a circle. The spider got down low and tried to squeeze beneath the rising door. The scorpion stood tall and raised its tail. The bullfrog jumped, knocking its head against the cage roof. The wasp stung the ground beneath its feet twice and the grizzly bear growled.

The crowd released several collective gasps.

God's People began stirring. Most stayed close to the cage but a few began to wander. Frail screams were released. Children buried terrified faces against their mother's dresses. Fathers cursed Jonathan's name.

"This is going to be good," Jon whispered.

A string of saliva dangled between Monk's thin lips, he looked terrified. And a moment later the spider squeezed its body under the cage door.

It was free. And it was Hungry.

∞∞⊙∞∞

Eight long, hairy legs scampered across the ground with incredible speed, creating a sound similar to a trotting horse. Each leg was the size of a tree trunk, orange on one side and brown on the other. It hard-shelled back was as thick as the bible.

It leapt.

Helga turned her lanky body towards the giant arachnid with her mouth gaped in fear and her tongue pulled so deep into her throat you'd think she was trying to swallow it. She stepped back, looking directly into three rows of eyes. From her perspective the eyes looked like a deformed face.

As the 750-pound spider knocked her down she couldn't help noticing that the creature smelled like a barn. The spider nuzzled closer. Its two front legs held her shoulders, two long, orange, mandibles snapped together, tearing away her face and half her skull. Helga's blood and brains spewed into the air.

Then all the people of Monk Town flinched and God's People started running. But there with no escape plan, only the need to move.

Four children stayed where they were, three girls and a boy.

The boy's eyes were glued in place. He watched the giant spider with his hands at his heart. If not for the fear in his eyes, he'd look like he had fallen in love.

Next to the boy, a girl with pigtails began pissing herself.

And next to the girl with the pigtails, a girl wearing a bright yellow dress had her hands over her eyes, her shoulders raised to her ears, and her elbows tucked into her waist. Her knees were pressed together, making her legs look like they were melting. She was whispering, "Stand still and nothing will hurt you."

On her left stood a two-year-old girl.

The two-year-old had baby-smooth skin, blonde curly hair, and wasn't much bigger than a newborn. She watched people running and the giant spider cocooning Helga, but she didn't understand what was happening and she thought she might be dreaming.

Then the 650-pound wingless wasp squeezed free of its cage and came straight for her, moving in a clumsy stumble. One front leg was broken and it was trying to fly, but with no wings it just couldn't do it.

Suddenly the girl with the pigtails and the girl with the yellow dress ran in opposite direction, each of them screaming. This caused the boy to snap free from his daze and fall on his ass.

Then the wasp attacked the two-year-old. It knocked her over and stung her right between the eyes, killing her instantly. With her head pinned to the earth, the boy could see blonde hair turning into red strings of goo.

∞∞∞⊙∞∞∞

Now that the cages were open, Bill Watt wondered if he would end up in hell. If so, somehow it seemed fitting. Opening the doors was a sin.

Looking down, Bill watching the rat step from its cage. Then a man named Davis Poppy (who wasn't exactly sure why he sided with God's People) ran directly into the rodent and quickly lost half an arm. "Oh Gawd!" He screamed with blood gushing from an elbow. Then his feet started moving and he ran towards the scorpion. The scorpion, ignoring Davis, scurried across the Pit and attacked the spider. In retaliation, the spider released a web that shot through the air and pinned Father Maloney to the wall. And as that happened, the rattlesnake slithered into Bill's field of vision and snatched up little Betty Whitman, swallowing the boy—shoes and all—in a quick, uncaring gulp.

Bill looked at the gorilla.

Its hands were two feet wide and three feet long. It's teeth were the length of a man's arm. The beast stepped from its cage with its head low, grabbed a woman and tore her in half.

Bill's eyes drifted.

Suddenly, it seemed, there was too much going on.

He saw a pool of blood in the center of the Pit. He saw spider webs spraying across a wall. He saw a string of intestines falling from the wolf's mouth. He saw a man with no legs crawling with his hands. He saw people running into animals, into each other, and into the cages. He saw a ten-year-old girl stumbling into the 850-pound lizard as blood poured from her mouth. He saw a six-year-old boy leaning against a torso with his guts lying in his lap. He saw a head-less woman falling to the ground and man that must have been stung by the wasp; his chest was so swollen that he looked like a bursting water balloon. He saw a man climbing the wall and a girl with an eyeball hanging from her head.

And these were people he knew, every one of them. They were friends and neighbors, the people of Monk Town.

Bill looked across the Pit.

Jonathan was leaning over the rail.

Monk was sitting in his chair, wondering if he had gone too far.

And below the two men, people screamed and ran in circles, looking for safety, looking for help. But there wasn't anywhere to hide. The Pit was just a big circle, a bunch of cages and pulleys and a gigantic locked door.

Nothing more.

∞∞∞⊕∞∞∞

Monk saw the 9,000-pound grizzly bear pounce on a boy's chest, flattening him like a manhole cover. He saw the wolf chasing the children, biting one boy in the neck, and thrashing him about. He saw the wasp leap onto the lizard's back and pierce the reptile with its stinger. He saw a man hitting another man with a severed arm.

Monk looked away. He wasn't sure how much more he could take. He said, "Shit Jon, are you seeing this?"

"This is unbelievable," Jon agreed, pointing. "Look at that."

Monk looked. He saw the rat standing in front of its cage, eating Davis Poppy's arm. He saw the wolf jump onto the rat's back and bite its throat; the rat squealed and rolled over with its feet kicking and its nose twitching. He saw the grizzly take a swing at the scor-pion, ripping the insect in half; white mushy puss emptied on a rope of webbing. He saw a five-year-old with no hand, screaming as blood poured from his wrist. He saw Ruth Huppert, dressed in her home-made sack, holding a child's head. He saw two women hiding behind the turtle, which was still in its cage and appeared to be sleeping.

"I don't know where you're pointing." Monk said.

"There, see! Look at the frog. See what it's doing?"

He looked at the bullfrog, which was jumping up and down, crushing things. He watched as it landed on the wasp, squishing the insect's white and green innards into paste. And when the frog leapt again it smashed the Pit's caged ceiling so hard that the building shook and the cage broke open.

The gorilla—being the smartest animal—looked up, pounded its chest and ran for the opening. The frog bounced again and the beast swatted it across the room.

Without hesitation all 650 paying spectators screamed in terror and made for the door. Absonoff got there first, followed by Keller and Norton King—but there was a problem. The door swung in, not out, and when people tried to leave they got congested in the doorway and the door became jammed.

There was no escape.

The gorilla crawled up the wall and onto the main floor. And when it saw the people of Monk Town, it attacked.

∞∞⊙∞∞

In the end less than fifty survived.

One survivor was the town's only scientist, Jonathan Weakley. He left early the next morning with his head hung low. Nobody said goodbye; nobody wished him well. Unwanted and unappreciated, Jon made his way to New York City with the status of failure. But he was no quitter; he had drive and he had ambition. He had hopes and dreams—*big* dreams. He was going to make something of himself; he was going to be a superstar. The world would look upon his creatures with wonder.

All that stood in his way would be punished.

ZOMBIES

THE HANGING TREE

Doc said, "Don't you play games, Red. The Hanging Tree is off limits."

Red snickered, gazing through the drizzle of rain, past the water falling in drips and drops from the rim of his leather hat. Looking into Doc's eyes he could see more than simple fright. He could see dread, as honest and true as the sky above them, and the nightly darkness that was on its way to conceal the town.

Hubert Turret, commonly referred to as Doc, looked more like a gunslinger than a doctor, standing at the side of the road with his black, rawhide jacket wrapped around his muscular body and his long fingers tickling the smooth, ivory-plated handle on his gun. He was an influential man, handsome yet rugged, capable of taking care of terrible business in desperate times, even when the business disagreed with him on a personal level. And tonight, that's exactly what the situation happened to be. It was terrible business and he wanted no part of it. Dealings were of the killing nature, which was never easy for *any* good-hearted soul, especially the likes of Hubert 'Doc' Turret. He was trained to save lives, not extinguish them.

He said, "The hanging tree—"

"The Hanging tree *was* off limits, Doc." Red Coltrane wasn't all that different from Hubert Turret. He was strong and lean, thoughtful yet commanding. He didn't enjoy killing, but did what needed to be done. It was in his nature.

He pointed a dirty finger at Mort Clancy.

Mort, with his knees planted in the mud and a noose wrapped around his scrawny neck, looked pathetic. He was like a mangy dog sealed up in a man's body. No effort put into his wardrobe, posture, haircut or hygiene. No attempt at being happy, healthy, respected or educated. He wasn't feared. He wasn't loved. He wasn't appreciated or hated. Add it up and what do you get? Not much. Just a skinny drifter with a neglected beard, a funky smell, and no one giving a rat's ass about his wellbeing.

He wasn't a bad guy, oddly enough. He wasn't dishonest or corrupt, but the fact of the matter was this: Mort wasn't the sharpest tool in the shed and more nights than not he earned himself the title of 'most likely to drink himself sick and pass out in the gutter.' Sometimes reputations are forged through exaggeration and fabrication. His wasn't. His was earned, night in and night out. If they handed out awards for boozing his mantel would be loaded with trophies.

"It *was* off limits," Red went on to say, still pointing at Mort. "Until *this* piece of shit decided to shoot Sheriff Gill."

Mort slinked away from the two men, eyes slithering from one to the other apologetically. He scratched his beard and snorted back a throat full of earthy phlegm.

There was no question as to whether or not Mort Clancy killed Sheriff Gill. Everyone knew that he did. He shot Gill inside *Good & Weston's Tavern* the previous night with a handful of spectators bearing witness. There was no reason for it, unless alcohol consumed was considered an incentive. After a few too many wiggly-suds he pulled his gun from his holster and shot the man point blank, right between the eyes. Simple as that.

Doc looked over Red's shoulder. His eyes skimmed the row of building on his left. There were more than a few faces behind the windows. He supposed they had a right to be curious. Killings and executions weren't exactly common in Ghoutan, population less than seven hundred and fifty. But they weren't exactly unheard of either. If he were inside one of those buildings, he'd be eyes to the glass as well.

Mort opened his mouth to speak, revealing cavity-rotten teeth that had been stained brown by twenty years of chewing tobacco and zero years keeping his mouth clean. "It was an accident," he mumbled without conviction. "I didn't mean to do it."

"Shut up Mort," Red barked, yanking on the free end of the hangman's rope. "I was there. I saw what happened and it was no accident. You killed him... now you're a dead man walking."

"That's what I'm afraid of," Doc scoffed.

Red forced out a laugh. "Oh... you're a clever one, aren't ya?"

"No. No I'm not. But there's a reason the Hanging Tree has been off limits for forty years, Red. Don't pretend there isn't."

"Forty years ago you were a child and I was nothing more than an inch in my daddy's pants. I might have believed those stories when I was *five*, but I sure as hell don't believe 'em now."

"Well I do."

"Well isn't that special. Good for you, Sunshine."

"No. Not 'good for me.' You've said—quite publicly, I may add—that Sheriff Gill was one of your best friends."

"That's right. He was. You can't work with a man like Gill without developing a friendship."

"Then why won't you respect him now?"

"*I'm* the sheriff now."

"I'm not arguing that. The task falls on your shoulders. I know it. *Everybody* knows it. But Red, I'm your friend too, and I'm trying to talk some sense into you."

"But you're not making sense!"

"Yes I am! Hang him in Town Square, the way it's been done for the last forty years!"

"No!"

"Why?"

"I don't want to hang him there! In fact, I don't want to hang *anyone* there. Town Square is no place to kill a man."

"Why not?"

"What do you mean, *why not?* You know why! It's right in the center of town. Everyone comes out of their homes and makes a big deal out of it. Taking a man's life shouldn't be a sport, Doc... *we're not barbarians*. We have over thirty children living within spitting distance of Town Square, and the bloody school is right next door!"

"A public hanging is nothing the children haven't seen before."

"That's the problem! Don't you get it? We've been making a spectacle out of these killings for too long! And why, because of an old wives tale? I don't want *children* seeing this stuff. Goddamn, I still remember it, Doc. I still remember watching my first hanging. I'll never forget it. I was four years old and the man's name was Jonny Bale. He was crying and terrified and his wife was screaming her head off, saying he was innocent, saying her man was a good man and he'd never hurt a fly. And when they pulled that lever, Jonny fell very hard, and every single person that was there heard his neck snap. It sounded like a bullwhip cracking; I swear it did. I had nightmares for a year, if not longer."

"Oh, bullshit."

"Don't give me that. It's not *bullshit*. It's true. And now I'm the man in charge and we're doing things *my* way. You want to hang this fool next door to a schoolyard? Why? So we can give nightmares to the young ones? No chance in hell. Mort's taking a one way trip to the Hanging Tree and that's final."

"But the Hanging Tree is… well…" Doc's eyes skipped towards the ground. "Don't make me say it, Red."

"Say what… haunted? Is that what you want to say?"

"I don't know if the tree's *haunted* or not, but you know what happens. Sometimes they come back."

The words sat in the air like an unseen hex, gaining weight as both parities had a chance to mull over the situation. They knew the stories. Everyone in town knew the stories, but that didn't mean that everyone in town believed them. Problem was, the stories grew more outrageous and less believable each time they were spoken. The Hanging Tree was cursed, many said. It always had been; some figured it always would be.

"Listen guys," Mort begged. "I don't want to die. I really don't. I made a mistake, that's all. It was just a stupid mistake and I'll never do anything like that again. Please don't kill me. *Please*. You could let me go. You could—"

"Be quiet, Mort," Red snapped. "If you didn't want to be executed you shouldn't have popped the sheriff. Good Lord, man. What were you thinking? Gill has a family, for Christ's sake. And he never did anything to you."

Doc agreed. "Yeah, shut the hell up. Now's not the time."

Although Mort had been told, he kept talking. They planned on killing him anyhow, so he had nothing left to lose. "All those years I walked the earth without a gun. I never needed one when I was a young lad, and I didn't need one now. But I got one anyhow, tryin' to be a big man, tryin' to be respected… and look at me! I *killed* the sheriff. Oh God, this isn't the way things are supposed to be! I should never have bought that *stupid* weapon. Lord knows a man like me shouldn't be armed. Gentlemen, please, set me free! I'm begging you! I could run off to a far away place, you'll never see me again. That wouldn't be too bad, would it? Nobody would have to know!"

"I'd know," Red said, using an unpleasant tone. "And so would Doc. Christ on a caboose, Mort. Sheriff Gill was a friend of mine. And I may not want to hang you in *Town Square*, but you're getting hanged all right. No question there. Your time on this earth is done like dinner. You shot a good man and a true friend; now it's time for justice."

Mort started crying. "Well for the love of God, don't take me to the *Hanging Tree!* I don't want to come *back from the dead!*"

Red said, "Don't be a fool, you won't come back."

"Yes he will," Doc argued. "You know he will."

"I *don't* know that he will. As far as I'm concerned, the dead stay dead."

"Not always."

"Yes. *Always.*"

"Well, I guess you plan on finding out for sure, don't you?"

Red huffed, flashing his teeth like an animal. "Look Doc, I'm getting tired of this. I need you to come with me, be a witness, and pronounce this man dead. If you're not interested, that's fine. I'll find someone else."

"We shouldn't be doing this."

"Is that a yes or a no?"

"It's wrong."

"Yes or no, Doc. I'm tired of getting rained on. I need an answer."

Doc squinted his eyes and dragged a finger across his chin. "Goddamn you, Red. I hope you're right."

"I am right."

"Okay then. Something goes wrong, it's your fault." And with that, Doc started walking, boots splashing in the muck.

"Get up Mort," Red said, tightening his grip on the hangman's rope. "It's time to move."

Reluctantly, Mort brought himself to his feet.

The three men walked towards a nearby stable with the warm August wind blowing at them from the west. At gunpoint, Mort mounted a mule. Doc and Red straddled strong dark horses, and together they made their way towards the place best left forgotten.

Twenty-five minutes later Mort was fastened to the tree in question, the one that had a reputation for giving death to the living and life to the dead. He was crying, afraid of what lie ahead, gripping the senseless mule beneath him with his heels. He was wearing a white shirt, which had become torn and covered in filth. His hands were tied in front. His glossy eyes were the color of cherry brandy.

The tree was old, more perished than vibrant. Its leafless branches were thick and knotted. Like giant, arthritic fingers, grasping at the open plains that surrounded it. Gluttonous roots burrowed deep within the mostly desolate soil, seizing nourishment where they could, keeping what moisture they found tucked inside, hoarding the sustenance, cactus like. In a different time and place it may have been called the *Tree of Anguish*, the *Tree of Shame*. Some thought that in days long since passed, in a time when the plant was truly alive, when leaves bloomed and sparrows nested among the branches, what existed was a rare and unnamed class of oak. Now it was impossible to know with any amount of certainty what type of tree it was, and the only birds to brave enough to wrap talons around the tautened bark were the buzzards and the crows.

Red ignored Mort's expressions of grief, turned to Hubert Turret and said, "I'm going to make this quick. Any last words, Doc?"

"We shouldn't be doing this."

"Your judgment and opinion has been duly noted." He turned towards Mort. "Hey Quick-draw. Quit yer crying a minute, will ya? I'm about to kick the mule. Have you got any last words, or are ya good to go?"

Mort snorted back what he was able and shook his head several times. A mixture of liquids ran from his beard. "Don't hang me from this tree, Red. Don't you dare... *please!* If this tree does what it was born to do, I'm going to come back. And if I do—"

"Yeah, yeah," Red said, uncaringly. "Is that it? That everything?"

"If I come back I'm coming back for you!"

Lightning cracked and thunder roared. The smell of the earth was strong now, stronger than before. It had been raining for hours, which was a rarity on the dry plains. The previously dehydrated terrain was thankful, more so now with the rain turning into a full-fledged storm.

Mort glanced towards the sky. Then, as tears rolled down his face, he said, "I mean it. I'll come back for ya. You'll be the first person I exterminate!"

Red heard enough. He kicked the mule until the animal moved away from the tree, leaving Mort swinging in the wind.

Gagging, Mort's eyes bulged. His feet kicked in every possible direction.

Lightning cracked again and Doc turned away. Red didn't; he watched the man suffer. Once the deed was done he made the sign of the cross, and said, "Want to pronounce him, Doc?"

Doc took one look at Mort's lifeless body swaying from side to side. He didn't need to be a doctor to know the score. Mort's eyes had rolled back. His terror stricken expression was locked in place. Limbs seemed boneless and somehow miserable. His white shirt flapped in the wind, reminding both men of a dirty flag.

I surrender; the flag declared. *There'll be no more trouble from the likes of me.*

Doc's eyes narrowed. He nodded and said, "Sure as shit, he's gone. May God have mercy on his soul."

"And ours." Red cleared his throat, pulled his hat from his head and placed it above his heart. After a moment had passed, he said, "Lets go back. We can send the meat-wagon first thing in the morning."

∞∞⊙∞∞

Sleep didn't come easy. Red's mind kept returning to the Hanging Tree. He could see Mort sitting on the Mule, crying openly, water dripping from his unkempt beard while his legs gripped the animal for stability. He could hear those words; *I'll come back for ya. You'll be the first person I exterminate.* Somehow Red believed it. But that was foolish, wasn't it? Sure it was. Mort wasn't coming back from the dead. That was impossible.

In time, Red closed his eyes and sleep came. It was a short-lived rest—a couple of hours, maybe less. He pulled himself from bed and walked towards the window. Looking out, he could see the rain falling lightly, splashing miniature explosions the puddles outside his window.

His mind drifted.

The tree. It all came back to the tree. He needed to see it again. Or more specifically, he needed to see Mort hanging from the tree again. He needed to make sure Mort was still dead. "God," he whispered. "I'm a fool."

And maybe he was a fool. But if so, he was a fool that knew himself pretty well. The next few hours were not going to be enjoyable ones. He was going to be awake, thinking about Mort, wondering if the impossible was somehow possible. This meant that he had a decision to make. He could either stay home, alone in his house, listening to the rain bouncing off his roof while he wondered if Mort was coming to get him, or he could go to the Hanging Tree and put his mind at ease.

After ten minutes of scratching his head and considering his options, the decision was made. He couldn't stay home, strolling from room to room while thinking in circles; it was making him crazy. He needed to go to the Hanging Tree and see Mort, whether it was a silly thing to do or not.

Red dressed, knocked back a tall shot of cheap whiskey and made his way to the stable. He mounted his horse and rode towards his destination. He rode slowly, apathetically. The air had cooled some. The ground felt soft from the rain, which had become almost nonexistent. Before he arrived at the tree he stopped to gather his thoughts.

Lord, give me strength.

Somewhere in the distance a coyote howled, nipping his prayers in the bud.

He dismounted, tied his horse to a nearby rock and began walking. He told himself that he needed time to think, but the truth was this: he was procrastinating. Seeing Mort's corpse hanging from a noose wasn't going to be pleasant, not at all. But what if there was no corpse to see? What then?

There was no easy answer to that question and Red didn't try to find one. Instead he continued on, hand on his gun, eyes on his boots.

The Hanging Tree was just past the roll of the next hill. Red walked the hill slowly. When he looked up he could see it, the tree. There it was, standing tall in all its glory.

Mort was—

Gone.

Oh shit, Red thought. His stomach turned and his knees became weak. *What the hell happened here?*

As his eyes expanded his footsteps slowed. Staggered. Stopped. Stepping back, he put his hand to his mouth. There was something on the ground, a dark lump beneath the tree. Looked like a body.

He took a cautious step forward, followed by another.

But what was it? Was the lump Mort? Could it be? Was it possible?

Suddenly he was running. He could feel his heart pounding in his chest and a cold chill crawling up his back and he was running. Heaven help him, he was rushing towards the unknown. It wasn't a conscious decision; it just happened. He needed to see what that man-sized lump was made of, because Mort lying beneath the tree meant that everything was okay in the world, everything made sense. The rope had become unraveled, the branch had snapped. Either way, something rational happened. And that's what he wanted—no... *needed*. That's what he *needed*. He needed something normal and sane, something he could wrap his brain around. A broken branch was rational. An unraveled rope was too. Mort Clancy coming back from the dead, on the other hand, was not.

His feet sloshed through the puddles. And when he arrived at the tree, beneath the knotted, leafless branches, he could see Mort lying there, face down in the mud.

Dead. He was dead. Thank God.

Red almost laughed, but the nervous sound that slipped past his lips didn't sound connected to humor in any way. Still, it was done. He had come to see Mort and he did.

It was time to go home.

Red blessed himself, turned away from the corpse, and started walking. Long before he made his way to his horse he began thinking about what he had seen. Something was wrong. Something didn't add up. There was no rope around Mort's neck, no broken branch either. And there was something else, something he couldn't put his finger on.

I need to go back.

But why go back? How would that change anything?

Because I missed something, he thought. *Something's not right.*

But what was it?

Red stopped walking. His shoulders slumped as he turned towards the tree. He could see the body beneath it, lying motionless.

Just go back, he thought. *Take one last look and head home.*

Halfheartedly, Red went back and stood next to the body. There it was: a dark lump beneath the tree. He kicked it and heard a groan.

The corpse groaned.

Oh shit. How was that possible?

The corpse groaned again, louder this time. Then it moved. Perhaps it was breathing. Perhaps it was about to stand up.

The color fell out of Red's face and the world seemed to tilt on one axel; for a moment he thought he might faint. But he didn't faint. Instead an inspiration came. *Run*, he thought. *Get the hell out of here!*

His feet stayed where they were, glued to the earth, next to the corpse, covered in mud.

Was it possible that Mort hadn't died? Was it possible that he was still alive somehow, that he freed himself from the noose?

No. It wasn't. Mort was definitely dead; Doc had confirmed it.

Red felt dizzy; he stumbled. And as he placed his hand on the Hanging Tree for balance, he felt something completely unexpected. His eyes opened wide and his muscles stiffened.

The Hanging Tree was no ordinary tree. Touching it was like placing your hand in a nest of rattlesnakes. It was alive somehow. Alive, but not like the other trees. Like an electrical current. Or a virus. And with sudden understanding came terrible knowledge. The roots of this atrocity didn't simply burrow into the earth; they tunneled into a different time, a different world—into the place where bad things come from. Was there life after death? Yes, there most certainly was. The Hanging Tree was proof, for its seeds were planted in the dominion of the dead. Planted in the world next to ours, not where the angels go, but in that region where all pain and suffering is eternal, where sins will never be forgiven, where hatred and revulsion are universal while sympathy and compassion have no meaning. The Hanging Tree was rooted in a land where evil deeds and sinful dealings fueled a never-ending flame.

Red pulled his hand away from the tree as if burned.

He remembered the hanging. He remembered the look of terror stamped across Mort's lifeless face, his white shirt blowing in the wind, looking like a—

"A flag," Red whispered.

But the corpse at Red's feet wasn't wearing a white shirt. It was wearing a black jacket. The same one Doc had on.

Red reached down, grabbed hold of the black jacket and flipped the body over. It wasn't Mort's face staring up at him. It was his gunslinger friend. It was Doc, who was clinging to death's front door.

With a scorched voice, Doc said, "Look out. He's behind you…"

Red heard something. Muscles tightening, he spun around.

Mort was there.

Mort, with the noose wrapped around his scrawny neck and his eyes glossed over, polished clean, lifeless, eternal. His skin was like melted candle wax. The stink of death crept from his throat and oozed from his pores. His filthy white shirt clung to his body like a second layer of flesh.

Red screamed, and reached for his gun.

Mort moaned and groaned, limped forward and extended both of his hands. He grabbed Red by the shoulder and pulled him forward.

Red managed to snag his gun from his holster. He stuck the barrel into the zombie's stomach and yanked on the trigger. The sound of bullets blasting through cloth, skin, muscle, organs, and bones, was earsplitting.

Doc opened his mouth wide. He leaned in. His yellow, checkered teeth tore into Red's neck, ripping his flesh apart.

Blood splattered across both faces.

Red tried to scream a second time, but only a desperate whisper escaped beyond his lips. He tugged on the trigger three more times quickly. He felt the zombie sway. He felt the teeth on his neck again and he stepped back. The heel of his left boot thumped Doc in the chest and his balance was lost. Suddenly he was falling—falling back, over his dying friend, tumbling into the muck beside the tree, bringing the living corpse down on top of him as his blood rivered from his wound.

Mort bit into his neck again, and again.

The fight inside Red was weakening; his desperation faded.

Light started to diminish. Vision blurred. Darkness came.

He was fainting. Or dying. He wasn't sure which.

Eyes fluttered, closed. It was over. Over.

Nothing left.

Nothing.

Noth—

Death.

Then it happened. Red felt something cold and terrible.

His glossy eyes opened. Someone had strung him up, and now he was hanging from the tree, swaying in the breeze, noose around his neck. He had been dead for hours.

But his thirst for killing had just begun.

THOUGHTS OF THE DEAD

Oh God. It's so confusing. More than confusing, really. I've got so much to say that I don't know where to begin. Maybe I should start with this: I've realized something while I've been sitting here, staring at the blank page. If they want me to recap my tale, which they do, then I want my words to characterize the real me, which is the *old* me—the guy people loved, the odd-ball funny dude that people phoned up and said, "Hey buddy... it's been too long; lets hang out." I don't want this cluster of words to simplify my life by representing nothing more than my recent problems, dilemmas and illnesses. I don't want these words to be bogged down in a sea of uncompromising negatives. I want to illustrate who I was, not who I am. I guess what I'm trying to say is this: just because I've—

Hold on a minute.

PLEASE GO AWAY.

YES.

YOU.

NO. BOTH OF YOU.

I'LL TELL YOU EVERYTHING, BUT I NEED TO BE ALONE
WHILE I DO THIS.

NO. I'M FINE.

I'M NOT TRYING TO BE DIFFICULT. I'M TRYING TO
COOPERATE, HONEST.

YOU'VE GOT TO UNDERSTAND HOW HARD THIS IS FOR
ME. YOU NEED TO STOP LOOKING OVER MY
SHOULDER. I CAN'T CONCENTRATE WITH YOU HERE.

PLEASE.

NOW.

YES, NOW.

I'M SURE.

WHY CAN'T YOU EMPATHIZE?

PLEASE.

OKAY.

OKAY.

SORRY, BUT MY WRITING IS FINISHED UNTIL
YOU GIVE ME THE SPACE AND RESPECT I DESERVE.

I'M WAITING.

STILL WAITING.

I'm back. Sorry about that.

I was going to tell you a few things but now it seems I have some explaining to do.

Right now I'm tied to a chair. Poorly. My arms are free but my legs and waist are not, which is silly. I could untie myself if I wanted; it wouldn't be hard. In fact, it would be easy. I won't untie myself though, and I suppose the men in the combat gear know it.

As weird as this may sound, I'm afraid to unravel the knots. I'm scared of what could happen afterward. Not to me, but to them. I know what I am. Oh yes I do. I know what I am; I know what I've done, and I know one thing for certain: I don't want to hurt anybody. Not again. Not ever.

There's an old typewriter sitting on the table in front of me. It's black and rusted and it looks like it weighs a thousands pounds. That's right. It's not a computer; it's a typewriter. Crazy huh? Can you say: BLAST FROM THE PAST - or - HISTORIC RELIC?

Okay, so… you're wondering why I'm writing this masterpiece on a typewriter? Yes? No? Doesn't matter. I'll tell you anyhow.

The city's power has been off for at least six months now. Conventional technology—such as computers, radios and televisions—have been, *ah*… how should I put it… *less than grand,* maybe? If you're reading my words you already know what's been happening in this messed up world of ours. So, why am I telling you things you already know? Why the pointless recap? I don't know. Bored I guess. Doesn't matter. I have to write something or the military guys will get mad.

There was an epidemic. Government officials said everything was under control. It wasn't. They called the disease the African Hyena Flu but the media dubbed it the Zombie Plague. I can safely declare the media's label a better fit. And do you want to know why? Sure you do.

Because—*and here it is, the million dollar answer*—I'm a zombie.

That's right. Sorry, but its true.

I was infected a little more than three months ago, which is to say that roughly ninety days ago I died and came back and I started killing my family, friends, and neighbors. And now—strange as it seems—I'm here, strapped to this chair, typing away, and trying to tap into the person I used to be.

Here's something that's a bit off topic: I'm wondering who will read this. Not just today, but over time. I know the assholes with the guns will read it, as will the doctors, but who else? I mean, am I writing something important here? I might be. Isn't that odd? These sentences might be *important*. Even if I write stupid words like 'poop' or 'cucumber' – they'll probably be analyzed.

Here's a word: RECTUM.
Ha! Too funny!

Huh.

I just re-read my last couple paragraphs and realized that I shouldn't have said the things I did. Not the rectum part – I like stupid jokes. *(Duh!)* I mean the other part.

The military guys are probably nice people. They're probably not assholes. And without a doubt they've been through a lot. Of course they have. I know it. And if I found myself in their shoes—lets be honest—would I act differently? No. Probably not. So for the record, they're not assholes. I'm an asshole for calling them names.

If you're reading this: sorry guys. My bad.

Wow. Back in the day… like, when the world was all about 'the typewriter,' if you wrote something it just sat on the page forever. You couldn't delete it or nothing. Very strange. I wish I could delete some on the nonsense I've been writing here. Oh well.

I'm rambling. Sorry again. I'll try to be less idiotic and more informative.

They put a needle in my brain, my temple—in case you're wondering.

That's right. A needle… a big one. Actually, they've given me a few shots in the temple now. And listen to this: as soon as they injected me that first time the crazy shit in my head cleared right up. The effect was damn near immediate. Isn't that amazing? If I had to describe the feeling I'd say it was the opposite of getting stoned.

Ever smoke a joint?

I smoked a few, back in my college days. Not many, but a few. What I remember most is that head-rush feeling—that spinning, tipsy sensation that comes a few seconds after you take your first drag. Well, when they stabbed the needle into my brain and pushed the medicine inside me, it felt like the opposite of getting stoned. It was as if my mind was already messed up, and the needle took the corruption away. I'm no doctor, so I don't know what happened to me *medically*, but I know that the fog lifted, if that makes any sense. And now that I think about it, once the medicine starts to wear off the fog will probably creep back in again.

Jeez. That's a bummer.

I didn't consider *that* until just now.

Huh.

Anyways—

From what I can tell there are about forty-five people here, inside this... whatever it is. I guess it's an office. Four physicians. Ten wounded. Another ten military and about twenty civilians—normal people like you and me. Well... not me. But you know what I mean. Plus there are fifty or sixty zombies kept in different cages. I was one of those, picked at random and given the shots.

Hold on.

PLEASE LEAVE.

I'M FINE.

NO. HONEST, I'M FINE.

I FEEL GREAT.

YES. THANK YOU.

PLEASE, GIVE ME BREATHING ROOM.

THANKS.

Sorry. They came back in, wanting to check up on me again. I can't say I blame them. I would have checked in on me before now.

Oh, here's something else I should mention: I have no tongue. I chewed it off at some point, which is why I'm typing instead of being interviewed verbally. This is also the reason (as I'm sure you can guess) I have to write my thoughts to the men in charge. If I could tell them what happened—or tell them to bugger off while I write this note—I would.

So, I've avoided reliving my personal story for as long as possible. I guess I should begin. After all, that's what they've asked me to do, and that's why they've put me inside this room: to tell my tale.

But really, I can't help thinking: what's the point? Is my depiction of tragedy going to be much different then all the rest? I think not. The fact that I'm writing these pages should be proof enough that the medicine they've given me is working, right? Isn't *that* the significant thing? I think so.

So, for what it's worth—doctors and scientists—the medicine is good. It's a little late in the game for me, though. In case you haven't noticed.

For those of you in charge: you should try your remedy out with the *recently* infected, give them the injection *before they die*. Or at the very least: shortly after.

A side note:

Do you know what I'm looking at?

My fingers.

Do you know what my fingers look like? Can you guess?

Let me give you a hint:

I've been dead for three months. My flesh is rotting. I've used my hands to smash through doors and walls, to break windows and dig holes, to rip apart throats, break bones and snag flesh from muscle. My fingers have shredded peoples ribs and faces and been dragged along asphalt. Not only that, but my wounds won't heal.

Now can you guess what my fingers look like?

I have no pinky on my left hand, no ring finger either. A zombie chewed them off. My knuckles are showing. Not the skin, I mean the knuckles. I have tattered piles of green meat bunched together in-between my fingers. My fingernails are all black and gray—except for the three fingernails that are missing. (BTW - I have no idea what happened to them so don't ask.) If I squeeze my bloated hands into fists, maggots fall like rain. I stink. Even *I* can tell how much I stink.

God… I am so disgusting now.

I hate to say this, but they need to kill me. I mean, like, REALLY kill me. Cut off my head or something, you know? I'm not in much pain, believe it or not. But I don't want to live this way.

Live. Huh.

I guess this isn't exactly *living* now, is it? Not with my heart sitting in my chest like a cold, dead frog.

Uh oh.

I can… I can feel the medicine losing its potency. Oh no, oh no. The sickness inside my brain is returning. Shit.

Know how I can tell?

Easy. The anger is coming back. I can feel the fury and the hatred bubbling just beneath the surface of my thoughts. The rage and tur-moil inside my body is growing. This is no good. I probably need another—

GET OUT OF HERE.

NOW.

NO, I DON'T WANT YOU HERE.

GET LOST!

Sorry. The military guys came back again.

What was I saying? Oh yeah. The medicine's effectiveness is weakening. This means—

Damn. I feel stupid admitting this, but I shouldn't have told the soldiers to leave. I should have asked for another injection.

Well, shit. Too late now. Next time they come in I'll ask for another shot. No biggie. I'm sure they'll return before long.

Where was I?

Oh yeah.

Okay. I'm going to tell my story before I lose my train of thought. I'm a family man. No, wait. Lets start with the basics. My name is David Kyle McClure. I'm a 38-year-old bus driver, or at least I was before the shit hit the fan. I'm six feet tall. I have short brown hair and a light skin tone. I like basketball; my favorite team is the Nets. I enjoy reading books by Dan Brown, Michael Crichton and Ian Rankin. My favorite type of music is eighties rock. Bands like Depeche Mode, The Smiths, Human League, The Cure…

Ugh. I'm not going to describe myself this way. It seems stupid somehow. I'm just going to… ah, never mind.

Let me start again.

For the past nine years I've been married to the best women in the world. Her name is Kathy. She's the love of my life and I'm so lucky to be with her. Kathy and I were married in California on a warm summer's day and we have two wonderful children: Tammy and Josh. Yep... that's right, a boy and a girl. Tammy's ten and Josh is – was – eight.

Damn. This is hard.

Okay... let me give it another shot.

My wife's name... was... Kathy.

Fuck.

I don't know if I can do this.

Oh crap. I'm starting to cry.

Give me a minute...

GET THE HELL OUT! GET OUT!

I'LL FUCKING TELL YOU WHEN I'M READY!

Sorry. I was just thinking about stuff, is all. For the last twenty minutes or so I haven't been typing anything. I've just been sitting here thinking about all the terrible shit that's happened to me.

It's not fair, you know? It's not. Everything is so fucked up; it makes me very upset.

Why am I the infected one, huh? Why me? Why not someone else? Why am I the one to have his fingers chewed off by that friggin' priest?

Oh yeah. I probably didn't mention THAT part of the equation, did I? That's right. A priest infected me! Kathy thought it would be a good idea to go to church. She said, "We might not be any safer but at least we'll be in God's hands." The kids were crying and I'd been awake for about forty hours and I didn't know what to do. I needed rest more than anything else in the world and she said if we went to church we'd meet up with other people and they'd be able to take watch for a while. I argued with her. I said it was a stupid idea but she kept complaining, again and again, until I finally snapped.

I said, "Okay honey! We'll go to that stupid fucking church if you'll shut your big mouth… but it won't be my fault if something happens. And guess what? Something happened! Zombies were everywhere and we were attacked before we made it to the bloody car! Oh fuck. If I had realized how stupid my dumb bitch of a wife was I never would have listened. Sometimes she makes me sick! I should have stabbed her with a fucking machete. I should have smashed her goddamn face apart with a hammer. I'm not kidding. I hate stupid bitches. I don't know why I ever married that fat fucking cow. I could have done so much better than her. I've hated her for years. She ruined my life, giving me those useless fucking brats. I should have left her. Or better yet, I should have demanded a pair of abortions and then left her.

I fucking hate my children, and I fucking hate stupid fat fucking know-it-all-sluts that think they're smart but are so goddamn dense they should fucking die. Bitches like Kathy make me furious! I wish I had smashed her teeth out and blasted the kids with a shotgun. I wish I had raped her ass with my fist and chopped her head off with an axe.

Want to know what happened? Listen to this:

I had Tammy's hand. Kathy had Josh. I opened up our front door and out we went. We didn't have a gun; we didn't have a knife. We didn't have anything but a GOOD FUCKING IDEA, right honey? Right, sweetie-pie? Right, love of my GODDAMN life? Yes. Of course that's right. And then what happened? There's no need to guess 'cause you know the fucking answer: out came the zombies! That's right! They were on the street, in the yards, between the houses. One jumped off the neighbor's roof!

Oh Kathy, why did I listen to you? You're a stupid whore and if you were here right now I'd snap your fucking neck. I'll cut your throat and drink your blood. I'd rip the eyes out of your head and stuff them up your goddamn cunt. I would. I swear it, I really would.

I don't want these fucking ropes on me. I fucking hate these ropes. They're making me furious.

I'm taking them off.

Otay. Where was I?

Oh yes. We were running to the car and these zombies came at us. I wish I could say that I didn't recognize any opf them but I did. I did reconizr= tehm. Howard Zolfo was there. He looked ;so fuckin stupid. He had hafe his face tornd off and all dis blood on his shirt. He was screaming and chewing on something and

GET THE FUCCK OUT!

GAT OUT!!!!

His shirt was bloodie and his face was filled wif scabs and he grabbed my boy. My stupid boy. I watched him snap my boyz neck with wif his zombie fingers aand I yelled don't but he did it anyways and what do i care? Joshs eyes turned whte and blod s plashd on the drivewey and I runned to the car and it was only my wife and me and my little gurl Tammy. They ate josh. I hate him and tammy so much that i started 2 cry when I saw that she had blod all over her face and her arm ribbed a part. I loved thm and ii hated tham and I runned over some people on the road when we were driving and some of them were zombies but not all of themm . some ware people. Like misses haper. I runned over misss s harper but ii din'tt meen two. i saw her head smash opan and i was crying and so was my wife and we went to 2 church but it was no better.

Preople weree screeming andd thay were fighing and the zombies were everywhere they took myn girl. They took tammy and she sad daddy! daddy whe I was trin to get tham 2 stop she sad daddy and they bit my fingerz. Iscreamed but it didn't matters. I watched my wife got biten and i killed the priest with my broken hands but it waz to latye. I was enfected. My lattle girl was rppid intwo pieces. Laterv that night iwas a zomboe i and aand I ddon'tb know n what happin next but ii was eating people and I kiiled my wif an she was good. she tasteddgood that tastedb like steaks aand I wants 2 eats morev= steaks cause-

i love killing i love killing i love killing love and ii chued my tongu off caz id was hungreee killm

di.d mjhr fin9877 an eatiung steajs zombies were averywhere aand ii was one oftham and i liked blood it and

soon they will cum inn

the door ands

they willl

IcOMEe

IN CoME Innn

I will kill them all ccccause that's whnat a zombie do. COME INN and ii ama azombie now now kkk kkkkkkkkkkkkill tham all rurf r rirqh ghhg gihgqr9qri'GjjjQcause now I like eatinkillingieat preole ii wants them 2 come in come inR;m 888ir9gpt hy bgpfaeo

trjhhnm h tirjs9' ;lg555o come In here come in. its ok if yuzs cum in kl.fv.sg fe;roqgo4 4fokfgq qf its okay if I kil u 84t87t5 ;;o89uq5 y4;5;I g5 5g' 'o53u q345ig '8888 cOMEe an iill kill u all kjrkgrlllll llllllll j k d heu r rh f8qf qi8 844p2 2< qp0` 4 fsssssssss442 22 2 -898 lngs npvw4urs eu e eeooroovrkkll llllllllll

iouqwehn9cy cp8yt4[0q 844hg ogo4 ;
n3f
jjjjjjjjjjjjjjjjjjjjjjjjjjjjjjjjjjjjjjjjjjjjjjjjjjjjjj

qqqqttw

SUMMER OF 1816

She was a writer who couldn't focus, couldn't think. The words on the page came slowly, painfully, if they came at all. After an hour and ten minutes, Mary Shelley, frustrated, lowered her head and dropped the pen from her hand, allowing the ink to drip. She slid her high-back chair away from the lavish table an inch, maybe two. She had no concept, no story. Inspiration was thin at best.

It was time to quit with the scribbles, call it a night.

The downpour of rain, the violent lightning, the excessive thunder. These things brought darkness and gloom, painting an image of misery while casting an enormous eclipse over the city. Tonight, like every other night this month, the storm was dominant, making it virtually impossible for Mary to maintain a level of attentiveness or concentration.

Would this storm never end?

Mary knew *why* the weather had become hostile: the Tambora volcano erupted in Indonesia three weeks earlier, dropping 1500 cubic kilometers of ash into the atmosphere. The explosion killed 10,000 people instantly, another 92,000 were killed by the eruption, and 82,000 died of starvation. In total, 184,000 people were dead. It was the largest eruption in historic time.

Mary knew these facts, most of them anyway. She put two and two together: big, bad volcano went big, bad weather. Simple as that.

Some thought the horrific weather conditions marked the beginning of the end: the apocalypse.

Somehow Mary doubted it.

Tapping her fingers on the table, an image floated within the constructs of her mind. It was the face of a friend, Lord Byron.

She closed her eyes, sighed.

Byron was losing his faith in her, and Mary didn't want that. Didn't want the man to mislay his confidence, his belief. The writing circle was all she had, or so it seemed more nights than not. And Lord Byron was the biggest part of the writing circle. If he lost faith, cast her aside, what then?

Expelling a deep and shaky breath, Mary visualized a smug look on Byron's face. She imagined him grinning and laughing. Then, without realizing it, her hands became tightly clenched fists and her knuckles turned white.

A horror story, Bryon had challenged.

Damn.

Shuffling her thoughts, she considered another friend, another circle member: John Keats. But Keats was no smarter than Byron. He was no better. Of course, he did have some good qualities. He was handsome, well dressed, well spoken. He had strong hands, wide shoulders, and a kind face. And she thought about Keats from time to time, when she was alone, away from her husband. When she felt needy, adventurous. Mischievous. But she didn't *like* him.

Or did she?

Mary wasn't sure.

John Keats didn't understand Mary Shelly's complexities. He never thought about her, never looked at her the way she looked at him, with ravenous eyes and fervent desire. No. John was too absorbed, and something of a character. He was slain by his own ego, his own designs—filled to the brim with self-esteem, pride and arrogance. And to make matters worse, John Keats *loved* Byron's idea of writing a horror story. He absolutely adored it.

Mary opened her eyes and unraveled her fists. She looked at the design of the stones beneath her feet and the mug of tea sitting next to her pen. She looked at the unfocused scribbles on the page. The word *disappointing* came to mind; her writing had become sloppy in more ways then one.

I want to stab myself in the heart, she thought uncharacteristically, while fighting the urge to scream out in frustration.

And then, without hesitation, Mary thought of Keats. Again.

∞∞⊙∞∞

"You solicit the darkness," Keats had said on the heels of Byron making his horror story suggestion. The words rolled off his tongue as if he were an actor in a play. His back straightened. His smile engulfed his face. "And I am but the spark to light that darkness, that malignant imp. A fine and justly wicked proposal. Excellent my dear man, austerely excellent."

Laughter from another room seeped through the doorway.

"Keats," Mary whispered then, thinking the laughter to be his.

She felt a knot in her stomach, and hated the emotions that messed with her thoughts. She had become as confused as a school-girl. Sometimes she wanted to embrace Keats. Sometime she wanted to strangle him. Sometimes she wanted to strangle Keats and Byron both.

Her eyes became thin, frightful slits.

They wanted horror…

It occurred to Mary, as she sat away from the desk, that her husband, Percy Shelley, had agreed with the horror story idea as well. He smiled with delight upon hearing it.

What was he thinking?

Was it not bad enough that Mary had fallen in love with Percy, a well-known, married man? Not bad enough that she was guilty of destroying his marriage and held responsible for his wife's suicide? Could Percy not see her misfortune, her heartbreak, her turmoil?

Did he not care?

Mary had *too much* horror in her real life. They all knew it. Why in God's name create more?

Her father had disowned her; her sister had committed suicide mere weeks ago—two closely related suicides in one year, no less. Her marriage was surrounded by fierce public hostility. She was driven out of town. And now, Byron challenges the writing group to create horror?

Horror?

Is he a fool, she wondered. *Or does he secretly hate me?*

With the question came fury, merciless and swift.

Sweeping the pages from the table, Mary leapt up and circled the room. Thoughts and words were complicated inside her mind no more. Her thoughts were flowing, burning. If she had an ax, she would split the table in two. No—in four! She would drop the blade as many times as she could, until blisters in her fingers were created and blood dripped from her hands.

Her muscles tightened; her teeth clenched.

Needing a drink more than she ever had in her nineteen years, Mary checked the cabinet on the far side of the room. Sometimes a bottle of wine would be there, sometimes two or three.

Today there were none.

Didn't matter. She didn't want wine. Not really. She wanted something harder, something cutting. And she needed time alone, time away from the group and the castle they were residing in. Time to think, time away from this hell she now called home.

The thought of sneaking off to the *Orchid Street Pub* had barely crossed Mary's mind when a snap of lightning lit the sky, illuminating the castle's giant wall of windows. She glanced through the glass and peeked outside.

Streets had become rivers. Valleys had turned to ponds. It was another intense August evening, muggy and humid, rainy and gusty.

Was a drink really worth the trek?

Mary crossed the room, approaching the hallway door with slow, cautious steps. She placed her ear against the thick of the door. Listened. Heard nothing, then voices. She heard Byron laugh, Keats laugh. She heard Percy speak.

And her small hands became white knuckled fists.

It was decided. She would go.

Tonight, Mary would leave the writing group in search of inspiration, and walk the dark and watery streets, alone.

∞∞∞⊙∞∞∞

He was a huge man, who looked like warrior, but served as a grave keeper. His name was Frank, and he sat alone in the *Orchid Street Pub*. His arms were pythons; his legs were tree trunks. He had an eye with no sight and a scar the length of a long blade around his neck. With four of his front teeth missing, he appeared to be the largest, meanest, man in Europe.

Some thought him to be the largest man in the world.

The cemetery, which sat less than one hundred and twenty yards from the small, empty pub, had the bodies of two men, a woman, and a child, rotting inside posh wooden coffins, deep in the basement of the yard's pantheon-style mausoleum. With each passing day, the stench of the dead grew more fetid, more rotted and foul. Rats, disfigured and diseased, would soon gather around the caskets in distressful numbers. This was no good. Graves needed to be dug.

Frank understood this, but was getting nothing accomplished. He couldn't work in this weather, and the storm had lasted three weeks now. It was growing stronger, getting worse, and stopping his workday before it began.

He swayed, and turned his head.

William the barkeep was sitting on a stool in the corner of the pub, cleaning glasses. He looked up, smiling. Then, keeping his hands busy, he eyed Frank, wishing that he would leave.

William didn't want to sit inside a near-empty bar. He wanted to be home, in the company of family. Of course, he would never say anything, not to a man of *Frank's* size. He valued his neck and guarded it watchfully.

Mary opened the door and stepped inside. She was soaked. Her clothing hung from her body like an oversized wet glove. Hair dangled in long, thin strands. Water ran from her chin.

She looks like a drowned cat, William thought, placing a glass on a table. He stepped behind the bar. *And she appears to be alone. How unfortunately odd.*

"My lady," Will said. "What brings you out on a night as dreary and as dreadful as this? Surely you can't be alone."

Mary shook off the rain the best she could. She pulled her hat from her head, slapped it against her leg, and made her way across the room. Sitting on a stool not far from Frank, she glanced his way, but did not see him.

"My only desire is to be out," Mary said to the barkeep, shifting her meager weight inside her sopping attire, "to be away from those who have cluttered my thoughts and dampened my heart. I am alone—here for the same reason that anyone would come to an establishment such as this, on a night so sodden. To wash the pain and grief from my tired mind, and drink my sorrows away."

"Aye," the barkeep said. "But to be a woman, young and alone? It is not common, nor is it considered wise. The necropolis sitting but a stone's throw away is teeming to the gates with brave young women, fearless women, women that died by the cursed ways of the streets."

"I would think it less wise to travel alone on a handsome night," Mary quickly responded, "a night in which the streets were thick with men, intoxicated men. Obtuse men. Tonight, there is none of that. There *are* no men. The streets are wet, I question that not. But the streets are safe enough for the likes of me. The pathway is innocent, innocent as it is apt to be. This I reckon to be true."

"Aye," the barkeep said again, seeing the wisdom of Mary's thinking. "Then, my lady of the storm, what shall it be? Perhaps an Irish tea to warm the blood?"

Mary smiled, ran her fingers through her dripping hair. "Perhaps a dry cloth?"

William smirked. "Of course. Let me check the back room. I'll find something for you."

"Thank you."

"Not at all."

As William walked away, Mary's eyes fell upon Frank. For the first time, she *looked* at him, really *looked* at him. His large, bulky stature sent a shock of anxiety through her body; he seemed more monster than man.

"My name is Mary Shelly. I live down the way."

The words fell from Mary's mouth before she knew she would say them. It was an act of nervousness, not bravery or desire for companionship.

Frank turned towards Mary. He rubbed his giant hand against his chin and grinned. "Are you not fearful of me, woman?"

Mary sat straight, wondering if she had initiated an unwise conversation. A moment passed. "Should I be?"

"Most are."

William re-entered the room and handed Mary a towel.

She thanked him, crushing the fabric against her body, hair, and face. She ordered a glass of scotch. William fetched the drink and Mary paid for it. A moment later, William returned to his stool, and lost himself in his work.

"You failed to answer the question." Mary said, after taking a pair of sips from her glass. The alcohol burned, and soothed, as she spoke.

"Aye."

"Well? Will you answer it?"

Keeping his eyes on his drink, the grave keeper said, "A woman should be afraid of what gives her fear, be it wise or be it not."

"Yes, of course. But should I fear you?"

Frank's eyes rolled in their hollows, like pool balls into a pocket. "Not of me. I know what I am. And what I'm not. I am a man of peace, not anger and violence. Fear me none."

"Oh?"

"Aye."

Mary took another drink. This time, the alcohol burned less.

"Then why, might I ask, do you have the look of a man that has seen a great deal of violence? Perhaps you were born with that scar around your neck. Is that so?"

"I was born with no scar," Frank said, his voice becoming quiet. He was not amused.

"So you *do* know violence."

Mary didn't know why she challenged the giant man. It seemed unwise, and yet for some reason, she enjoyed playing with danger.

Frank could see what Mary was doing, the way she was manipulating the conversation. He didn't like it, and he began to ignore her.

He drank from his cup. In time, they drank together in silence.

Frank ordered another drink, as did Mary. William filled both glasses and returned to his work. Then Mary eyed Frank one last time, baiting him with her stare.

And still, Frank didn't budge.

Mary thought her little game with the giant was over, and after she had given up all hope of conversation, Frank surprised her, saying:

"I have something that would fill your heart black with dread, woman. You need not fear me, foolish girl who walks the streets of a thousand murders – *alone*. But I do hold a key, be it physical, *and* metaphorical. It is the key to the greatest fear I have ever known. It is the face of the serpent, the true hand of shadow."

In mid sip, Mary froze. She lowered her glass, turned her head and swallowed. Her eyes were round and wide. Her lips briefly quivered. "What did you say?"

"You know what I said, woman. You heard my words, and know their meaning."

"The hand of shadow?"

"Aye."

"The face of the serpent?"

Frank nodded, grinned. "Aye."

Mary expelled a great breath. Putting an arm on the bar rail, she whispered, "Lucifer? Lucifer of the fallen angels?"

Frank pulled himself away from his drink, seeing Mary with the only eye with which he could see.

He shrugged.

"Where?" Mary snapped.

If Frank had consumed less alcohol, he would have said nothing. Instead, he spoke without considering the consequence. "Not here, woman. In the mausoleum."

"You lie." Mary quickly spat, with anger growing inside.

"I do not lie."

"You do! You wish to lure me there—to bury me, after having raped and killed me! I am a scholar, and not easily fooled. I know the likes of you and your kind. You are not a man. You are a beast!"

Frank had had enough of Mary's insults. He slammed his hand on the bar, spilling his drink. "You've asked me if I'd seen battle, and I did not answer. But I shall answer you now. Yes! I *have* seen battle. I see battle every week of my life. A man my size can know not peace. I am a target, a marked man. I am the man others wish to knock down, to prove themselves men. They come at me often, drunk and brainless—like *you* woman, like you. They come alone at first, then in packs. The violence... it's always the same. I find bloodshed and carnage waiting at every corner around which I turn. I long for peace. I swear it, I do. But I shall never find peace. Not with the likes of you, and not until someone strikes me down. I shall not find harmony and serenity until I am dead, though my heart longs for its calm and tranquil shores. I pray for a life of peace, though I shall never get it."

Seething with anger, Frank turned away, wanting to smash something.

Mary gasped. She was speechless; she was touched. The giant man was no ogre. He was intelligent, educated and passionate. He spoke like a scholar, a teacher, a poet. Seconds passed, and Mary felt the overwhelmingly bitter sense of shame. "A book should not be judged by its cover," she said. "Nor should man. I am sorry, and ashamed. You have done nothing to make me believe that you are a creature of violence, yet it was the conclusion in which I arrived. I feel a fool."

Frank groaned like an animal. He said, "Don't bother. This cross is mine to bear, not yours. Just leave me be."

"But a man does not choose the size to which he grows. He grows until the Lord commands it not."

"I suppose."

"It is true. I've known it, and yet I was blind. Blind like a bat in the night. Again, I am sorry, truly sorry."

"Forget it woman. It's nothing."

Mary finished her drink, and William poured them another. Time passed. Then changing her tone, she said, "The face of the serpent?"

"Aye."

"Will you show me?"

Frank closed his eyes. If Mary had been nicer no him, he would have said *no*. Instead, spite encouraged a nod of his head. "Aye."

Mary shifted her weight, moved closer. "How can I be sure that your intentions are pure? I am a young woman, of nineteen years. I have been called beautiful. Most men considered noble would find themselves swimming with impure thoughts."

"I am not most men."

"Yes, yes, of course. But how do I know?"

Frank swallowed half his ale. "William!" he said. "Come."

William slipped off his stood, and approached the couple. "Another ale to warm the gullet?"

"No."

"No?" Will seemed puzzled. "Then what is it?"

"You know me?"

"Aye, that I do."

"Be truthful now. Do men, women, and children, fear me?"

William leaned back; stroked his chin lightly. "You are a man of great stature, of great physical strength. I believe they fear you."

"You've seen me fight?"

William nodded. "Aye."

"Have I ever picked a fight, picked one with a man that did not ask?"

"No. Not one. Men seem drawn."

Frank glanced at Mary. "Have you seen me harm a woman, or a child?"

"I have not."

"Am I known to *be* a man that harms women, children?"

"No." William said. "You are not."

"Thank you William."

"Not at all, Mr. Stein. Would you like another ale?"

"No thank you. I believe we are finished here. Isn't that right, *woman*?"

Mary bobbed her head. "Aye."

As William returned to his stool, Frank said with a doubtful tone, "I am to show you then?"

"The hand of shadow?"

Frank tapped a dirty finger against his dead eye. "The face of the serpent."

∞∞⊙∞∞

They walked through the burial ground as rain bounced off the tombstones, created lakes, drowned the grass, and drilled holes in the mud. Frank led the way, finding the highest ground, where the ponds were shallow beneath his feet. They approached the mausoleum, which sat near the center of the cemetery.

Made of sandstone, the building was a considerable size, larger than most fair-sized houses. Trees and shrubbery were plentiful around both sides of the structure. Headstones were also abundant, separated only by Christian statues and stone pathways. Smooth, slippery steps led to a six-pillar entry, centered by a tall black door with a long brass handle. Some thought the handle looked like gold.

Frank approached the door and produced a ring of keys, also made of brass. As he shuffled through them, Mary waited patiently. Frank found the appropriate key and slid it into the keyhole.

They stepped inside.

The crypt was a great hall with several rooms on each side. The air was musty, stale, and polluted with the stench of death. On the floor, mice scattered. Against the wall, unlit torches sat bundled together on a shelf, next to a dozen long, hand carved matchsticks.

Frank lifted a match from the shelf. He dipped it into a small asbestos bottle, which had been filled with sulfuric acid. The match ignited. Using the tiny flame, he lit a torch, and handed it to Mary. Then he lit another torch, which he kept for himself. The burning torches revealed an elaborate portrait on the ceiling. The stones became an ever-changing flicker of cherry red faces and beautiful landscapes, the toils of an unknown artist.

Frank walked past the empty rooms, and approached a staircase.

Mary followed.

"To the basement," Frank said, running fingers through his sopping wet hair. He briefly pulled his shirt away from his body, hating the way it felt.

"Is it here?" Mary asked, with a growing sense of fear.

"Aye, that it is. The face of the serpent is in the cellar, near the base of the stairs. As you may or may not know, this crypt was a jail in secret for many years. Or so it has been said."

"Not a secret. I've heard those rumors since I was small. This is true of a great many mausoleums."

"But things are different now. I've worked the grave a long while, and known not a single man kept in the dungeons of this place. That time has come and gone, it seems. Until…"

"Until now."

"Aye."

Mary coughed twice, and stroked her fingers along her dress. "The hand of shadow, this is a man in a cage?"

Frank grinned. "It is no man. But there is something locked in that cage. In fact, there are four of them."

"Four?"

"Aye. Four demons. Spawned from hell, the dark abyss, with skin rotting and eyes washed in the depths of fire. They don't breathe. They don't eat. They don't talk. They just wait, observing the living as the skin rots from their bones. And oh, how they moan, it sounds appalling, abysmal."

Mary looked shocked. Her mouth hung wide, like her jaw had been broken. Finally she snapped her lips shut, and said, "How did they come to be here, these creatures of anguish?"

"They came on the day the storm began, all of them. Loved ones brought three. The other came from the hospital. They were just people then, dead people. Nothing new for a place like this. I put each body in a coffin when it arrived, as I always do. A service was given in the rooms upstairs. We do that sometimes, if the weather is bad, or if it is requested. We charge more for an indoor service so it is not called for often, and when the storm breaks, which usually takes no more than a day or two, we bury the deceased in the yard with the others. But in that time between the service and the burial, we keep the bodies downstairs, locked in a cell."

"Locked? Why locked? They're dead, are they not?"

"Yes, of course. But from time-to-time there have been thieves. They break the door, come for jewelry, or the gold in their teeth. At some point I stopped leaving the corpses upstairs. I bring them to the cellar now, and lock them away." Frank giggled without happiness. "This time, something peculiar happened. Perhaps the storm brought it on. I do not know. Strange time this is. No dead since the storm arrived. None that I know of, anyway."

An odd droning hum came from the basement.

"What is that?" Mary asked.

"It is the dead. They have opened their eyes, woman. They have risen." Frank sighed. "I know not why you've come this far. You must be mad. But it is not too late to turn away. Satan has not seen your face yet."

Mary huffed. She wanted to leave, but needed to see. "Can I leave whenever I decide to?"

"You can leave now. I shall not stop you."

"No. Not yet. I long to see. I need to know."

"I know why *I* come here." Frank said. "I come to see that all remains well, but you? Why? Why place yourself within the grasp of a demon? Do you not fear your soul to blacken, your heart to wither?"

"You would not understand."

"But I would."

"No!" Mary said, louder than intended. Immediately she wished she had remained silent.

"Have I instilled no trust in that mind of yours? Am I so obtuse?"

"No."

"Then why would I not understand? Is it because I am a man?"

Mary wondered what to say, what to do. And she was afraid. If Frank wanted to hurt her, it would be easy now. No one would see, or hear. Help would not come. She was alone with the giant, and at his mercy. He could tear her head from her neck with his bare hands. He could snap her arm like a dry stick.

Mary shuffled her conflicting thoughts.

Frank seemed trustworthy. She sensed no hostility from him. He was another tortured soul, like she was. He was an innocent, and locked inside the prison of his own body. She hoped.

"If you must know," Mary whispered, as if the demons in the basement were listening, "I am a writer on a quest, in pursuit of inspiration. I've been asked to write a horror story, but find that I am without insight. My mind works in tragedy, for mine is a life of misfortune. My sister died three weeks ago, and still I cannot summon a tale of horror. If you were to show me the face of the serpent, the hand of shadow…"

"You will write it."

Mary winced. "Perhaps, perhaps not. Seeing the hand of shadow is not a tale in itself. There is no love interest, no conflict. I need inspiration, not obscure news banter."

Frank nodded, turned, and walked down the stairs. "Then my dear, you shall see the true face of horror."

∞∞⊙∞∞

Mary followed along, entering the basement upon heavy legs. She heard growling, and moaning. A putrid smell made her stomach turn. Reaching the bottom step, she realized that the rainwater had made its way inside somehow: The floor was littered with puddles.

Frank lifted his torch. He nodded, and turned away.

"Are you to leave me?" Mary asked.

With the sound of her voice, the moaning and growling stopped dead.

"Yes. The demons are here. They remain secure. That is all I need to know. Do not stand close to the cell, and you shall remain unharmed."

Frank disappeared up the stairs.

Mary took a step. Then another. The cell was within an arm's length now, but she could see nothing unusual.

"Hello?"

No answer. Silence.

Mary moved closer than Frank had suggested. She held the torch against the bars, and felt a chill. The cell seemed full of ice.

Then a boy appeared. He moved without speaking, without breathing. His fingers were long and thin, his stomach was bloated. Recessed eye sockets were drawn and dark. Ten years old and soulless, with skin that had turned from light and fair to black and purple. The eyes were red, shocking red, like glistening orbs of blood.

Looking into those eyes, Mary could see that the boy was not human, not now. He had the pupils of a demon, a serpent. Nothing from this earth could lurk behind those chilling red orbs, those deep haunting spheres.

Looking closer, Mary realized that she was not looking into the eyes of a single demon. She was looking at hundreds of demons—perhaps thousands, millions—all living inside the corpse-child together.

And *he* was the cold one. The chill was coming from inside of *him*.

Mary stepped away.

A man and a woman crept forward. Both were stinking, rotting. It was obvious that the man had been killed in some type of accident: his head was split open; the gray matter from his brain had leaked down his neck. The woman was tall with long dark hair, her dress was torn open; her wilting breasts were exposed. Rope marks circled her neck.

The corpse woman grinned. Pointed. She began to laugh with a multitude of voices. Her voice was a carnival of living death—an eerie rattling grind, a handful of sticks pressed against the slow moving spokes of a coach wheel.

Mary's eyes widened. Her legs felt weak.

"No," she said, her tone overflowing with pain. "Dear God, no! This cannot be!"

A forth corpse approached, limping on a broken leg. It lifted a gnarled hand as murky dribble flowed from its tattered mouth.

A moment later, Mary ran for the staircase screaming.

∞∞∞⊙∞∞∞

Frank waited by the front door for his guest to return. It didn't take long. Within two minutes she came to him. Her face was shocked; her skin looked bleached.

Frank said, "So, Mary the brave, the fool, did you find what you were looking for? Did you find inspiration, deep inside the tomb of the living dead?"

"That I did," Mary replied, with a trembling voice. A shaky hand wiped tears from her cheeks.

"Will you write the first great novel of horror, or was this blackening of your soul for nothing?"

"I do not know, nor do I care. I found more than I had bargained for, inside that cursed cellar of yours. I care not if I write another word. This event has shaken me to my very core, my foundation."

"I warned you."

"No, Mr. Stein, you don't understand. The woman in the basement, the one that had been hanged; her name is Fanny Imlay. She is my sister."

∞∞∞⊙∞∞∞

In time Mary thanked Frank, left the mausoleum and walked home alone. She was already wet, so the rain didn't bother her. However, the dark roads and alleyways did. She kept thinking that *something* was watching her.

Something dead.

It was a little after one in the morning when Mary arrived home. She entered through the castle's back door, the servant's entrance. She had left it unlocked.

A fresh change of clothing and a dry pair of shoes later, she was in her room, safe and sound. No one realized she had left. The entire event took less than three hours.

After tidying her desk and lifting the scattered paper from the floor, Mary placed a fresh sheet of paper in front of her and surrounded herself with candles. She dipped her pen into her inkbottle, smiled nervously, and began to write:

It was on a dreary night of November that I beheld the accomplishment of my toils. With an anxiety that almost amounted to agony, I collected the instruments of life around me, that I might infuse a spark of being into the lifeless thing that lay at my feet. It was already one in the morning; the rain pattered dismally against the panes, and my candle was nearly burnt out, when, by the glimmer of the half-extinguished light, I saw the dull yellow eye of the creature open.

She wrote those few words, no longer caring about Keats, Byron and Percy—what they were thinking, what they were saying. Her inspiration had been found. The first paragraph had been written. And a year later, in May of 1817, Frankenstein was completed. It was published January 1, 1818, and although she didn't know it then, her words would outlive them all.

Author's note:

Much of this story is true: the volcano eruption in Indonesia that killed 184,000 people, the weather surrounding the summer of 1816, Mary's writing circle (which included John Keats, Lord Byron, Percy Shelley), Lord Byron suggesting a horror story, Mary's sister's suicide (Fanny Imlay), Percy's ex-wife's suicide, Mary's age at the time, and the quote at the end of the story, which comes from the novel Frankenstein, Chapter IV (the first words Mary had written) is all true. However, some liberties were taken while establishing motivation, characters, relationships, and more obviously—the conclusion of the story.

FALLEN

Alex Greenly stumbled across the rooftop, dragging his tired and weary feet. The winds were strong but tasted sweet. The roads and alleyways in the city below had become a true a nightmare. Rotting flesh and unrestrained disease had progressed far beyond the point of intellectual capacity; being at ground level was like being trapped in a noxious abattoir while off fighting off a pack of rabid wolves.

He eyed the structure's edge cautiously; then circled the perimeter. Aching muscles screamed in protest. He needed rest.

Peeking over the building's edge, he could see birds flying. Cars looked like toys. The living dead swarmed around the building like locust.

If I jump, he thought, *it'll be over.*

His stomach turned and churned at the notion.

He didn't want to jump, not even a little. But he couldn't go on living like this. Who could? Maybe if he had a gun he could blast his way free of the metropolis, but he didn't have a gun. He didn't have anything.

This was the end and he knew it.

The rooftop door swung open and five of them came shuffling out, one after another. They were the living dead—starving, violent, infected, and insane. The first three moved in: a fat man with entrails hanging from his belly, a child with his jaw torn free, and a woman with three bullet holes in her forehead.

He wondered why the bullets hadn't stopped her, but the answer was simple: this wasn't a movie.

As Fat-man lunged forward, bugs fell from his mouth and his exposed intestines slapped against his knees. The woman howled at this, scratching a mound of shattered fingers against the worms in her chest.

Turning away from the zombies, Alex's knees buckled. His eyes closed. "The count of three," he whispered, extending both arms and hands. "One. Two…"

Eyes creeping open, he looked at his wedding ring and remembered his wife Samantha. Oh man, he loved her so much. If only—

Fat-man clamped Alex's shoulders and bit deep into his neck. Blood and maggots squirted across both faces.

The pain was colossal.

The corpse bit him again, and again.

Screaming, Alex pushed forward. With his feet slipping over the edge, he fell awkwardly. His ribcage slammed against the building's ledge as he tumbled over. He was plummeting now, falling seventy-two stories. Blood gushed from the severed artery in his neck like a high-powered fountain, speckling the building's wall.

He was dying; this was the end.

The absolute—

The infection, swimming inside his bloodstream, caused him to unleash a growl.

A powerful gust of wind slammed his body against the building. Bricks shredded his face; his nose exploded. A window ledge clipped his elbow and tore off an arm. Clipping his chin on another protrusion, his neck broke, and his head slammed into his back. Teeth flew of his mouth.

He died. And a moment later his eyes re-opened.

He wanted to kill, wanted to eat.

Then he hit the ground.

SCI-FI / FANTASY

THE RELATION SHIP

Inside a dream a boy played with his friends on the infinite shoreline of an undefined sea. He was happy, as were his friends. The games they played were always fun and exciting. They never seemed to end and they never grew tiresome or old. Then one day, between games, the boy left his friends and ran towards the shore that had intrigued him so often. He ran with a smile on his face and the speed of youth. He stopped just shy of the water's edge. He placed a finger knuckle deep in the water and then quickly pulled it away. The sea was cold and not at all pleasant.

The boy watched the waves crash against the shore relentlessly. His smile faded until his joyful expression was drained from his face. Each wave the boy investigated had come at a cost; the fee was his frame of mind. The waves made him feel lonely and despondent, which was a strange and surprising contrast to the games he commonly enjoyed; they always felt fun and cheerful. *But there's something fascinating about the waves*, he thought. *Something dangerous and exciting too.*

After a long while, the child returned to his friends and took his place among the activities. But his feelings had been altered now; he kept thinking about his finger stirring about in the cold water, for the sea had a strength and depth that the motionless beach had failed to provide. Each wave was mysterious and unique, having obtained its origin in an unknown place.

The boy turned away from the other children and looked at the sea once again.

Standing before him was a serpent named Lilith. She had dark hair, dark eyes and soft features. She had long legs and tight breasts. Her lips were full and her waist was thin. She seemed to be filled with joy—and looked nothing like a serpent.

"Perhaps you and I could travel the ocean together, child." Lilith said, with a subtle melody gliding within the magic of her voice.

The boy blushed, for her beauty was extraordinary and unsurpassed. "I don't understand," he said, feeling intrigued and embarrassed by his own imperfections.

"Do you not grow tired of the games? Are you not curious to see what adventures are awaiting you there, across the horizon?"

She pointed towards the sea.

"Yes," said the boy, still astonished by Lilith's splendor. "But I do not wish to travel out there, for the ocean—if that's what it is— seems to be a terrible and lonely place. I can't imagine happiness in a world with so much turmoil, so much death and destruction."

"Death and destruction?" Lilith asked, amused. "But whatever can you mean?"

"Do you not see it? Do you not see that each wave comes towards us vibrant and filled with power, only to be destroyed as it reaches the sands? What kind of place is the ocean, if it is not a place filled with sadness and pain?"

"My child," the serpent said, with a grin that seemed larger than her face. "Come with me. Let me enlighten you."

She led the boy away from the other children and the games they played. He didn't seem to mind.

"Where are we going?" the boy asked.

"I saw you standing on the shoreline with your finger in the ocean. Thoughts of adventure and excitement have set camp inside your mind. I know this, but hear my words: I judge you not. I understand your dreams, needs and desires, for I have them too. You and I are not so different."

The boy looked into the eyes of the serpent, amazed.

As she led him to the water, she said, "Adventure always comes with the risk of danger, but the risk need not be great. You and I possess something that you have not yet realized, and whether you realize it or not, this thing that I speak of is something we share together."

"What is it?" the boy asked, wide-eyed and confused.

Lilith smiled and considered her words carefully. "We shall build a ship together, and sail above the water. We shall remain dry always. And with each day that passes the ship will grow stronger and larger until you have forgotten all about this beach and the games in which you've played. The boat will become your home, the world shall be your backyard, and this place will be but a grain of sand within it."

As her words spilled from her lips she reached into her pocket and pulled out a small wooden cone that was shimmering with light as if energized. Its base was no larger than a fair sized coin; its point was sharp and radiant.

"Do you know what this is?" she asked.

The boy shook his head; he did not know.

"This is Love Zero, the physical manifestation of what some scientist call 'negative energy'. In simpler terms, this little entity is the first indication of a ship—a very special ship—one that grows if you and I allow it. Believe it or not my child, this undersized unit is something that you and I created together, just now. Without your involvement it shall remain like this—an object so small that I can conceal it in the palm of my hand." She crouched and put the tiny gleaming timber into the water with the flat side up and the pointed side down. Then she looked at the boy and smiled.

"Give me your hand child," she said.

The boy dropped to his knees; the sand felt very soft and warm beneath them. He placed his hand inside of hers. Without hesitation, Lilith put the boy's finger upon the cone, next to a finger of her own. The cone, glowing brighter now, began to expand. Soon it grew into a raft large enough for both to stand on.

The boy shook his head in amazement.

Lilith grinned like a shark. "Won't you join me on this adventure built for two?"

They stood up, hand in hand. The boy squinted his eyes and allowed his mouth to fall open with an expression that suggested he was deep in thought. Finally he said, "This is amazing. It truly is, I have never seen anything like it; but what if I don't want to join you on an adventure built for two? Don't get me wrong, I'm not saying that I want to stay here; it's just that… this is all happening so fast. My life is here; my friends are here. This is my birthplace, my home. This is the place that I know best."

"If the two of us do not step onboard, the cone will remain this way forever—a Love One. That is what you and I have created here: a Love One. It is much larger than it was when our eyes first met. It was a Love Zero then, and before that it didn't exist at all."

"Where did it come from?"

"Each time a person lays eyes on another they are given a choice. They can communicate and create a cone, a Love Zero. Or they can choose not to communicate and create nothing. You and I exchanged thoughts and words and we created a Love Zero. Then we put our hands together with a common purpose, creating a Love One. And now we're given a comparable choice once again. We can step onboard and generate a Love Two, or we can leave it be. But understand this: once a cone is created it can never be un-created. Once it is developed it can never be un-developed. It can be destroyed but not undone.

The boy was terribly confused by the serpent's words, but he loved the way that she spoke. She had the voice of an angel, or perhaps a goddess. He said, "How can the cone be destroyed? Will the ocean destroy it? And what about my friends, can they come with us?"

"The goal is not to destroy, but to create," Lilith said. "And the ocean can do no harm. If we join together the cone will grow into a great ship and each day it will grow larger and stronger until it becomes a huge vessel. The craft will be sturdy enough for as many friends as your heart desires. It will be sufficient accommodation for every person you have ever met, but for now, the craft is too small. It is only large enough for you and I."

She stepped onto the raft, which seemed sturdy and strong.

The boy hesitated, and then he followed her onboard. He sat down and pulled his knees to his chest, away from the waves around him. He looked across the sand, eying his friends nervously as they played their carefree games.

The serpent put her hands in the water and began to paddle. The beach fell away in the distance. And although it seemed strange to the boy that his beautiful new friend should be able to place her hands into the ocean without showing any signs of discomfort, he never thought to wonder why.

∞∞∞⊙∞∞∞

The years came and went, and the raft grew into a great yacht—greater than the boy could ever have imagined. It had tables, chairs, and places to relax. It had a kitchen filled with all the comforts a boy could wish for: a sink, a stove, a refrigerator and all his favorite food; it had a toy room, a workbench, a bathroom, and a pool. It had everything he wanted and more.

The boat was sturdy and strong; it was large enough to hold all of his friends and have them play every game they had ever played. But his childhood games were forgotten now, and all his friends were gone. The boat was his new home, just as the serpent said it would be. The beach had become a grain of sand inside his memory.

These things did not bother the boy—who was nearly a man now—for he had a new home and new memories to look back upon. And all of these memories—in one way or another—included his one-and-only friend, Lilith.

But Lilith was a different type of friend. She was very close to him physically, mentally and emotionally. And Lilith liked to play games that were unusual; games that made him feel like a jar of butterflies had been released inside his belly, games that kept him thinking about his new friend long after she had fallen asleep beside him.

Morning, noon, and night, they were together. Some days the fun never stopped; they laughed and laughed and laughed some more. And other days things were okay, not fun really, but routine. Truth be known, some days things were a little dull.

The young man was not concerned by days that felt dull. He had gotten used to them—slowly, during his time on the boat, and he felt content.

Then one morning, while the couple was in bed, Lilith became unreasonably angry.

The young man didn't understand why. Nothing inside the boat could have made the serpent so upset and unhappy, for the boat was a grand spectacle of luxury. It was something the two of them had built together. It had brought them joy and happiness most every day for the last few years.

And yet, here it was. Lilith was angry.

She yelled, and the boat made a strange noise.

The young man looked at the floor beneath his feet, for that seemed to be where the noise had come from.

"What was that?" he asked, with his eyes large and frightened. He wondered if the boat was under attack. Perhaps there was a shark in the water, or a whale, or a great creature with giant ship-crushing tentacles stirring beneath them in the deep. For the first time in his life he found himself worried about the vessel's wellbeing.

"I don't care what it is," Lilith responded.

He could see she was not joking. Lilith did not care. She was far too angry to care about a noise from below and she continued yelling, and cursing, and soon she was screaming.

The boat made another strange noise, followed by another. The bizarre sounds were getting louder.

As the young man became upset, Lilith unleashed an ugly grin. With the eyes of a snake, and a smirk holding no joy or happiness, she showed her anger, her resentment and her distaste. She was ugly, not beautiful like he had first thought.

"I'm sorry to interrupt you, my one-and-only love," the young man said, sitting up in the bed. "But I think it's best that I look in the basement. I should see what is making that terrible and fearsome noise."

"You will do no such thing," the serpent replied. "Or you'll discover how angry I can become! This fury is but the tip of an iceberg––one that is far deeper than you can imagine. You'll stay here with me and do as I say. I command it! Or learn the true depths of my rage."

Just then, the boat made another unnerving sound, which was followed by the swish of rushing water.

"Oh dear," he cried. He jumped out of bed, tugged his pants over his legs, and squished his feet into his shoes. "It's the boat! It's sinking! It's sinking!" He ran for the door.

"Don't run away while I'm talking to you!" Lilith screamed, "We're not finished here yet!"

"But my love, I must go, otherwise all will be lost! The sound of incoming water is too much to ignore! My heart is yours, so please forgive me."

He ran down three flights of steps, with his knees high and his feet soaring. He rushed into the boat's massive hull, exhibiting a speed he had never known.

Lilith continued screaming: "Get back here, dammit! I demand it!"

The hull was flooding. There were six separate holes; freezing cold water poured through each with an uncompromising force. The boat groaned and grumbled; then a new stream of water began pouring through a fresh opening in the wood.

The young man felt powerless as he searched the vessel for a toolbox. He found the tools inside a closet on the second floor, beneath a box of clean towels and new blankets. He returned to the hull as quick as he could and found that things had gotten much worse. There were so many holes that counting them was impossible.

Water had risen above his knees and was getting deeper by the second.

He smashed a bench it against a wall. Then he hammered nails into the wood, patching the places the water flooded quickest.

The patches held.

He smashed more furniture and patched holes for an hour, but it was no use. There were too many openings and the boat was sinking faster than ever. If he were to save the ship he needed Lilith's help. He could not do it alone.

The young man ran up the stairs and raced into the bedroom. "Lilith, Lilith, come quick," he said. "Our ship is sinking!"

After he spoke he realized that she was not there. The room was empty.

She must be helping, he thought.

He ran floor-to-floor, room-to-room, searching for his one-and-only friend. All the while new holes were created and the ship took on more water. Finally the young man checked the upper deck. He found Lilith bathing in the sunshine with a drink in her hand. To his surprise, she was not alone. She was with another serpent, a man serpent. He too was sun bathing and enjoying a drink.

It seemed sinfully wrong that Lilith should be having a cocktail with an unexpected guest. The boat was sinking.

The introductions and explanations would have to wait, the young man decided. "Our ship is sinking, my one true love. I need your help."

Lilith laughed. "I won't help you," she said. "Why should I? This vessel either stays afloat or it doesn't. If we sink, then it was meant to be."

"What are you saying?" the young man asked, quite honestly amazed that his one-and-only friend cared so little about the ship they had created together.

"You heard me."

"But why? You and I built this ship from nothing. It was a Love Zero; remember? And look what we have created!"

"If you wish to keep patching, than do so," Lilith said. "I won't interfere, with that I give you my word. But don't expect me to lift a hand either. I don't care enough to assist. If we go under, so be it."

The young man gasped. "You don't care enough to assist? But this vessel is all we have! How can you not care?"

Lilith shrugged and locked hands with the other serpent.

Seeing this, the young man's stomach burned. It was as if all the butterflies inside his belly had died a horrific and unforeseen death. "Are you with him... somehow?"

"No," Lilith said. She smiled and looked away. "Of course not. Don't be silly. He is just a friend."

Suddenly the young man understood her words, her lies... and the position he allowed himself to be in. He felt angry enough to put his fist through a wall. And for the first time since they had met, he saw how ugly Lilith really was, inside and out. She was a serpent.

But of course, he had known this all along.

∞∞∞⊙∞∞∞

The young man ran down the first flight of stairs. The bottom half of the boat was flooded now. His toolbox, which was in the hull, was lost.

He fell to his knees and cried, and his knees began to ache.

The ship is nothing like the beach, he thought. *It is hard and cold and ungiving. The beach is freedom; the boat is a prison.*

He heard footsteps, followed by a giggle and a splash.

When he checked the deck he found that Lilith and her new friend were gone.

An hour later the ship sank. The young man, feeling lonely and sad, held on to a broken piece of bench and drifted alone in the cold, undefined sea. In the distance he could see a cone shaped raft built for two.

Lilith and her new friend were on it.

SUFFER
SHIRLEY GUNN

Shirley Gunn dragged herself from the loneliness of her double bed and put on a pot of coffee. It was early, 6 am. Once the coffee was brewed she sat in her favorite chair, mug in hand, watching the sunrise through the large bay window in her living room. The town was uncommonly quiet; the streets were empty. Her dog, Blueberry––a beautiful and friendly, chocolate brown, Labrador retriever—was happy to see she had joined the land of the living. He sat close to Shirley's chair, his tail wagging excitedly.

Shirley smiled and the dog licked the back of her hand.

"Good morning, Blue."

The dog took a few steps back, stopped wagging his tail and lowered his head.

"Oh, what's a matter, boy? Shirley said, before slurping from her cup. "You want me to take you for a walk, don't cha?"

Blue wagged his tail twice more but his heart wasn't in it. The animal seemed to be carrying the weight of a troubled mind. If Shirley didn't know better she'd think the dog had been scolded.

She patted Blue's head lightly and smiled.

The dog nuzzled into her embrace; then quickly pulled away. And with a great sigh, Blue grinned a terrible and bewildering doggy grin, and spoke. "Shirley my dear, you and I need to talk."

The coffee mug slipped from nervous fingers and fell to the floor beside the chair. Coffee soiled the rug. Shirley's mouth cracked open and her eyes widened. Her bottom lip quivered and both of her hands began trembling. Her stomach, which had felt fine a moment ago, churned like she was trying to digest a toilet filled to the brim with concrete cement.

The dog talked.

"Oh Lord," she said. *The dog talked!*

"Don't be frightened, Shirley. There's no reason to fear me. You're my friend, my master. We've been living together since I was a pup, running in the yard, biting at your shoe. I stood by your side during your divorce and your depression, and slept at your feet when you were alone. I'm with you now, Shirley Gunn. You're my master, and you're my very best friend."

Shirley put a hand to her mouth and gasped. "You can talk!"

"Yes," Blueberry said. "I can talk. So, listen to my words… you are in great danger. We both are."

"How can you talk?"

"I'm afraid that conversation will have to wait, because at this very minute—"

"No! You need to tell me! How this is possible? You're speaking *English*, for crying out loud! Do you hear what you sound like? My God! You sound like my old University Professors!"

"Shirley, listen. I have some important things to—"

"NO!" Shirley slammed her fist onto the arm of her chair. "Tell me! HOW. IS. THIS. POSSIBLE?

Blueberry lowered his head in defeat. "Fine, don't get mad. I'll tell you."

The dog walked towards the window and looked up and down the street nervously, with paws gripping the carpet. When reasonably satisfied with the look of the neighborhood, he said, "Dogs are not what you think they are."

"You're an alien," Shirley whispered, more to herself than the dog. "You're from another planet, like that stupid movie with the…" She tapped her fingers against her temple, as if doing so would stimulate her memory.

"No." Blueberry said forcefully. He turned away from the window, but stayed close to it. "I'm not from another planet or a figment of your imagination. I'm a robot. All dogs are robots."

"All dogs are *robots*?"

"Yes."

"That's impossible."

"It's true."

"My last dog—Nightingale—was hit by a truck. I was there. She bled all over the street."

"Yes. I know she did. Look Shirley, I have to tell you something that is far more important than the history of your pets."

"Are you telling me that Nightingale was a robot?"

"Yes."

"This is crazy."

"I can understand why you might think so, but let me remind you—"

"Then why in the world did she die, right there in my hands? I was holding her. I watched her die. Her blood was all over me, and the road, and the truck that killed her! I... I can't believe I'm having a conversation with my dog! I've lost my mind, that's the only logical answer!"

Blueberry growled in frustration. "Every dog has a chip—"

"So if I cut you open right now, you won't bleed. You'll be all wires and electrodes inside, is that right?"

"No. If you cut me open I will bleed and it'll hurt like hell. Would you shut up for a minute? For God's sake, please, let me talk! I've put off talking as long as I can. I have some important things to tell you. And yes, I get it. I understand how shocking it must be for you, hearing me communicate this way, but get over it... at least for now. Okay?"

Shirley sighed. She looked at her dog, then at her feet, then at the mug sitting on the floor. Everything seemed different now. The world had just changed. "Okay," she said. "Sorry. I'm going to get myself a fresh mug of coffee and then you can tell me everything. Please, stay where you are... I need a moment to myself."

She got up and walked across the room in a daze. Her mind was reeling but her feet moved slow. This was a page from the Twilight Zone.

Blueberry waited patiently for his master to return. His eyes were locked firmly on the road.

Shirley returned several minutes later looking like she had cried. She had a fresh coffee in her hand. Her eyes were puffy and her skin was pale.

Blue said, "You ready?"

Shirley sat down, slurped her coffee, and closed her eyes. A few seconds later she opened them; nothing had changed. "Yes," she said insipidly. "I'm ready."

"Good. A great many years ago, before the ice age and before the Silurian period, there was civilization. There was intelligence, and technology, and science—do you follow me so far?" Blue was talking very quickly.

"Yes."

"Does it seem impossible that things evolved before several ice ages had a chance to destroy the developments of evolution, and erase the planet's progress from historical knowledge?"

"No. In fact it seems logical, if not likely."

"Okay. That's what I like to hear. Things evolved. This was well before the evolution of man, remember… and things were very different back then. I don't have time to explain how different, so please don't ask. Not now, okay?"

"Okay."

"Thank you. There's something inside my head similar to a computer chip. I'd tell you that it's man made, but it's not. It was created by hands, not completely unlike your own. The hands were of a class known as the Jappared. The Jappared is one of the species that ruled this planet before you. The chip they developed is small, much too small to see. Think of it like a computer chip, or memory card, hiding inside my DNA. All dogs have them, all wolves too. Now here's the important thing: the moment I opened my mouth and began talking with you a signal was sent to the other animals, to the dogs and the wolves. They know that I've broken the rule of codes, see? Which is a very bad thing to do. They see me as a virus now, an illness inside the computer's mainframe that is threatening to destroy their way of life. They'll be coming soon."

"Why?"

"To kill us both."

"Oh my Lord! Why… for crying out loud, why?"

"I'll explain everything, but look at yourself, Shirley. You're wearing your slippers and pajamas. You need to get changed. We need to get going."

"Where?"

Blue looked out the window again. The street remained quiet and empty. "Shirley. I'm going to say this once, and I hope you listen to me. GET DRESSED NOW."

Shirley's mouth slinked open. She looked outside, realizing that the danger wasn't metaphorical or spiritual. Not this time. It was physical. She could almost see the dogs of the neighborhood barking furiously as ignorant masters stumbled from bed to let them outside. She imagined the wolves of the north growling with lips snarling and fangs exposed.

She thought about the Boxer that lived next door. It was big. *Very* big.

"I have to get dressed," she whispered.

Blueberry nodded unwearyingly. "Yes you do."

"I spent too much time making that second coffee."

"Absolutely."

Shirley leapt from her chair and raced across the room, holding her drink in her hand. She dropped the cup on a table. She hustled free of her pajamas and into fresh clothing. "Where are we going?"

Blue stayed close, ready to move. "Bring your keys. We're heading to the car."

Shirley pulled on her running shoes without tying them, grabbed her purse, and made for the door. "I'm not sure where my cell phone has gone. I always leave it here, on the table—"

"Trust me… we don't have time. Forget about it."

Reluctantly, Shirley said, "Okay."

They stepped outside and hurried along the driveway. The morning air was nice and pleasant, spoiled only by the two Doberman pinschers that were coming down the street, looking like they were ready to kill them.

"Here they are," Blueberry said, lifting an eyebrow.

"Where?" Shirley looked down the street and saw the dogs immediately.

Each dog weighed close to eighty pounds. Ears were cropped. Legs were muscular. They ran with muzzles pulled back, teeth exposed, and eyes focused on Shirley's neck. They weren't barking or yelping. Their padded feet galloped along the pavement quietly, not drawing unwanted attention.

Shirley opened a car door, Blue piled into the backseat, Shirley jumped into the front. She slammed the door, started the car, and put it in gear before the Dobermans arrived. Then one leapt onto the hood, growling hungrily with incisor teeth exposed. It was easy to imagine the animal ripping a person's stomach apart and chewing on their entrails. The beast was born for killing.

"They're not barking," Shirley said.

"No," Blue admitted shamefully. "They won't."

The dog moved a little closer to the windshield, still growling, eying its intended prey. It didn't blink or lose focus in any conceivable way.

"Why not?"

"Barking is something we do to create an illusion. When a dog barks, it's for show. Even if the animal wants to hurt you, barking is just an act. It makes us appear less intelligent."

"I don't understand. Why would—"

Blue interrupted boldly. "You need to start driving, Shirley. The other dog is almost certainly chewing on your wheel. This is dog is creating a diversion. Nothing more. Never underestimate a dog's intellect."

Shirley felt as if her blood had turned cold.

She looked into her mirrors. Sure enough, the other dog was gnawing on a tire. Swallowing back a nervous shriek, she put the car into gear. One Doberman stepped away while the other jumped from the hood, landed softly on the asphalt, and slowly walked along the side of the car.

Both dogs watched as the car drove off.

Blueberry released a little doggy sigh, and said, "Oh boy. That was close; there's so much I need to tell you."

"Where are we going?"

"Huh? Oh, to your work."

Shirley turned her head and looked at Blue with her mouth gawking. "My work?"

"You're a scientist, right? You're one of the planet's top minds."

"Well, I don't know about *that*."

"You're high up on the food chain, are you not?"

"I'm connected, but it's been through hard work, not brilliance. I've never been at the top of my class. Not once."

Blue nodded.

Shirley rubbed a hand across her face, stretching her skin. She said, "First of all, you should sit in the front seat."

"You hate when I'm in the front."

"Yeah but… its different now. You're allowed."

Blue nodded, understanding. "Thank you."

They came to an intersection and Shirley had no choice but to stop behind a white pick-up, unless of course, she wanted to start driving around the truck and through the red light; she didn't. Blueberry leapt into the front seat and got comfortable, sitting with his back straight. A dog walked across the road and stood between the two vehicles, sniffing and growling. It was a mixed breed with no tags, lean and strong. The hairs on its back stood directly up. It didn't bark or make sudden movements. Its unclipped tail didn't wag. The dog seemed to understand that it couldn't get inside the car.

Shirley watched the dog nervously, then something caught her eye: Another dog, another mutt. Its long dark hair was shaggy; its paws were filthy. The area around its mouth was wet and smeared with something that looked like dark red jelly. It walked towards the car, eyes primed for battle.

When the light changed from red to green the first dog stepped out of her way. The truck turned right and Shirley drove ahead quickly. She wanted to ask about the dogs on the street, but had another question that seemed more pressing.

"Why are we going to my work?"

"We have a problem, a scientific one."

"Go on."

Blueberry licked his snout. "I said something like, 'all dogs are robots', right? Well, my statement wasn't completely accurate. The truth is, all dogs are *not* robots. All dogs are ONE robot. We're part of a collective. We have different lives and different temperaments, but we are one in the same. Think of us like different parts of a single computer, working in wireless harmony with a collective goal and a communal objective."

"Which is?"

Blue looked out the window and huffed. "You probably don't know this, but the human race isn't the top of the food chain. We are."

Shirley released a nervous laugh. "Yeah, right."

"Tell me, what does a King do?"

"I don't know…"

"Let me enlighten you. A King sits on his ass, and his slave wipes it. Understand?"

Shirley didn't understand at first, then her fingers began to tighten around the steering wheel and her stomach started to clench. She turned her head, looking at her pet through fresh eyes. She thought about the money she had spent feeding him and the countless times she picked shit from the yard. And for the first time ever, Shirley was mad at her dog. "Yeah. I guess I do understand."

"Don't be upset," Blue said. "It's just the way it is. And yes, I'm aware that all dogs are not treated like Kings. The ones that are treated poorly endure their misfortune for the greater good."

They drove over a rolling hill and spotted five more dogs at the side of road. Four were rottweilers, brimming with teeth and muscle. The other was a bulldog. The animals turned their heads, watching the car go by.

"Is it just me, or is there more dogs around now?"

"They're tracking us."

"How?"

"They have a wireless connection to me. It's impossible for me to escape them."

"What if I remove the chip?"

"It would be comparable to a doctor removing every blood cell."

Shirley nodded. In time, she said, "You didn't answer my question. Why are we going to my work?"

"I'll explain the situation the best I can. You ready?"

"I suppose so."

"Okay. Here we go: in the days of my creation there were a great many conflicts, achievements, and wars. The continents were laid out different, so life forms squabbled over different landmasses. In today's world we have achieved a universal checkmate, in a sense. If you blow me up, I'll blow you up. But in my day our focus was different. Our relationships with other life forms were different. Earth didn't have one dominate species, it had thousands—all advancing in different ways with distinctive concepts and idiosyncratic values. I was created to give beings a glimpse into the thought process of an intelligent life form, very similar to plant life. And through the evolution of technology I became something more, something unique… my own identity. After a while I was modified, not by the Jappared, but by a species called the Kudduu. With their help I became the most highly advanced machine in my mass category, which was a big deal back then. It is because of my insignificant size that my life form is here today."

"But… you're a dog."

"No. I am complex. I am a tiny chip that is millions of years old, enclosed in a warm-blooded husk, endorsed by beings that dwarf the aptitude of mankind one thousand times over. I am something that engineers itself inside the DNA of newborns, much like a natural life form does. The only difference is… I was built."

"Okay. I'm going to pretend that I understand completely…"

Blueberry looked out the window, trying to find the right words, the easiest words. "Think about this: the human race has done a bunch of strange and reckless things over the years, yes?"

"Absolutely."

"Well, so did we."

"The world is about to blow up? Is that what you're about to tell me?"

"No, not at all. But something bad is about to happen. There have been five separate ice ages; four that mankind know about, and one that mankind does not. I was built after the Cryogenian period, 590 million years ago. There have been three separate ice ages since then, the latest one occurring in the Pleistocene era, but that's not the point. Point is—the rulers of my day did something very terrible and very stupid."

Blue stopped talking, licked his muzzle and lowered his head. His eyebrows did that thing that only dogs are capable of... shifting towards the sides of his head, creating an expression of absolute sadness. He looked like he had been a *Bad Dog*.

He said, "They created a synthetic life form deep inside the moon. They worked on it for decades; it was very controversial, very experimental. Most thought the idea was insane. Others thought it was the greatest experimentation of all time, and in many ways it was. They set a timer to keep track of the creature's progress, but the timer was never meant to advance into maturity. And after a few thousand years, when the wars began and the planet started to look like it was going to flip on its axis—which, by the way, it did, but not then—nobody cared about the thing that was growing inside the moon. You see Shirley; they used the sun as an incubator and the moon as an egg's shell. Something has been growing inside the moon for 590 million years, a creature the size of the planet—and it's about to hatch. Do you mind opening a window?"

Wrapping her mind around Blueberry's words, Shirley felt faint. She hit a button and the window lowered. Blue stuck his head outside and let his tongue hang. After a few seconds the dog licked his snout and sat back inside.

"Thanks" Blue said. "You can close the window now."

Shirley did. She put a hand to her brow and said, "I'm sorry—did you say that something is growing inside the moon?"

"Yes."

"What is it?"

"I don't know. A monster. Something you've never seen before; something that will crack the moon open, stretch out its claw and destroy us on a whim. I would never have spoken to you about it, ever. It goes against my programming, but so does extinguishing my way of life. You can see the paradox, can't you? All dogs feel the end getting near, but I was living with you—a scientist. I was put into a position of choice. Talking with you conflicts with one element of my programming while remaining silent conflicts with another."

They arrived at Shirley's office. The building was large and the parking lot was filled with cars. She used a card key to get inside the parking lot, and said, "Look at the vehicles that are here early today. Why so many, I wonder… I would think that after a four-day week-end the staff would be dragging their butts and coming in late."

Blue shrugged. "I don't know why they're here early, but this is good news. We need people to see me, hear my words, and understand what I am telling them. We need people to start acting now, even if it means the end of the silence era."

Considering Blue's words, she felt inspired.

The end of the Silence Era.

Shirley grinned. She seemed to be involved in something big, something historical. She was at the forefront of a discovery that would change the planet forever. The story of her day would be written about and talked about in every communications medium around the world. She was about to be famous. Her voice was about to be heard.

Shirley parked close to the door; there didn't seem to be any dogs around.

She said, "You still didn't answer my question, why did we come here… to my work?"

"Let's go inside," Blue said. "I'll explain everything once we're safe."

They stepped out of the car and walked across the parking lot quickly, keeping an eye on their surroundings. When they got close to the building a pack of pit bulls came running towards them. They must have been hiding in the parking lot. Most of the dogs weighed in at about a hundred pounds. None looked friendly, and they seemed almost rabid with excitement.

Shirley and Blue ran the last few yards. Shirley was screaming, suddenly overwhelmed with fear. Her fame and notoriety would be short lived if these animals killed her. When they arrived at the door the doorknob was missing. It had been chewed off. Shirley stuck her fingers inside the hole where the handle had once been. She pulled; the door opened freely.

Something was wrong; she could feel it in her gut. She didn't want to go in there, not even a bit.

The pit bulls were almost on top of them now.

"Move!" Blue said, running past her legs.

Shirley reluctantly jolted inside and slammed the door.

The pit bulls stopped at the door, growling and creating a barricade. They snapped their teeth wildly but didn't attempt to enter the building.

Looking through the door's window, Shirley did a quick headcount. There were sixteen dogs at the door, maybe seventeen—several more were standing in the parking lot.

She moved away from the entrance and the animals that guarded it.

At the end of the corridor something was piled close to a wall; it looked like a flattened bag of laundry. They approached it slowly, cautiously. Blueberry first, Shirley a few steps behind. They walked past numerous doors and windows. There was an open wallet lying on the floor. Something was definitely wrong here.

They walked on.

Lying in a grotesque lump was a body; it looked male. The face had been gnawed and chewed until the skull had become crushed. One hand had been torn free from the arm. The shirt, no longer clean and white, had been ripped to shreds and intestines hung through the fabric. The pool of blood surrounding the corpse didn't expand too far, but as Blue and Shirley moved closer, the signs of battle became more apparent. There were plenty of large paw marks; an abundance of gore was splattered against a wall.

Shirley put a hand to her mouth, thinking she might be sick. Her stomach heaved and she leaned over, struggling to keep her nausea inside. In time she looked up, hand against the wall. She felt her knees tremble.

Four wolves were in the hallway, approaching slowly. They were full size, coming straight for her. She turned around, only to find five coyotes advancing from the opposite direction. This pack moved quicker, they looked hungry and mean.

Blueberry and Shirley were trapped.

"What should we do now?" Shirley asked, a quiver in her voice.

Blue strolled towards the wolves like he didn't have a care in the world. He licked his snout, and said, "I have another worker for you. She's not armed. I disposed of her cell phone last night. She might not realize it, but she left her purse in the car. This is Shirley Gunn; she was scheduled to arrive at 7:30 am. We are nearly forty minutes ahead of schedule. Hopefully this doesn't conflict with your timetable."

One wolf nodded. "No problem. This is fine."

Another said, "Nice job."

"Thank you," Blue said. "From the reports I've received, Ballistic Lane has terminated close to sixty percent of its residents. By tomorrow it should be ninety five percent secured."

"Very well," one of the larger wolves said. "We can handle it from here. Clear the hall."

Wolves and coyotes surrounded Shirley.

A wolf with ice-blue eyes said: "You have two choices, Shirley Gunn. You can come with us or die like him." The wolf nodded towards the lump on the floor. "Your choice."

Shirley looked at Blueberry; her face was masked in terror.

Blue said, "Sorry Shirley, but it's like this now." He turned away and walked down the hall, talking with one of the other animals, never once looking back.

Blue-eyes growled at Shirley, nudging her ahead.

Shirley walked through two hallways and up a flight of stairs. She stepped over two more dead bodies. One was a man she recognized; he worked on the same floor but in a different division. He was young, twenty-nine—just a kid really. Mark Blunt. He had been working with the company less than a year.

The wolves and coyotes brought Shirley to an office, forced her inside, and stood watch by the door.

A Great Dane, sitting between two slope-back Hyenas, told her to sit down.

She did.

The Great Dane said, "I don't know what lies you were told, nor do I care. I'll break things down for you, once. You live here now. The world you know has ended. Food will be supplied. You'll work in maintenance until you get transferred. You'll be assigned a partner for the first week of your stay, or until you have a solid grasp of your duties. If you talk with anyone aside from your partner, you will be terminated. If your work is sloppy or careless, you will be terminated.

If you create problems in any way, or if you try to escape, you will be terminated. If you cannot grasp your duties, or perform them adequately, you will be terminated. Do you understand? This requires a yes or no answer. Answer no and you'll be terminated."

Shirley reluctantly said, "Yes. I understand."

"Very good. You are dismissed."

The wolves led Shirley through a large room and down a well-lit hallway that was lined with corpses. She was placed in a fair-sized office and given a workstation next to the window. On her desk was a note. It said: Suffer Shirley Gunn. It seemed to be a statement about her future.

Click.

Shirley turned her head. A woman had locked the door before taking her seat on the far side of the room. She had blood on her shirt and make-up smeared down her face. Her name was Gwen White.

Shirley had known Gwen for years.

A man approached from the far side of the room. He was older, maybe sixty, sixty-five. He had cuts on his face, and three of his fingers had been chewed from his left hand. He said that his name was Louis; he had been assigned as her partner.

On the table before them was a dog, a German Sheppard. It rested on its side. It was neither moving nor breathing. The animal had a four-inch square panel embedded in its ribcage. The panel was open. Shirley saw nothing organic, just mechanics.

This was not an animal.

This was a machine.

Shirley looked out the window, thinking about Blueberry—the dog she had raised since it was a pup. She thought about the good times they shared, and the things he had said. She wondered who had created Blue and why. She wondered how many lies the dog had told her, and how many truths were hidden within those lies. Most of all, she thought about the moon. She marveled at its size and questioned whether or not something was living within it, something that was capable of destroying the earth on a whim.

Perhaps there's something living inside, she thought.

It was something to wish for, something to hold onto.

DARK HUMOR

HUMPY AND SHRIVELS

Late one night in October, two men sat in a bar, drinking beers and talking about the ever-changing weather. One man had a hump on his back the size of a medicine ball; his name was Gusto. The other man had a shriveled-up arm and a shriveled-up leg; his name was Hubert.

Gusto drank a mouthful of ale from his iron mug and rolled his right shoulder around in a slow moving circle. He dragged the back of his hand across his lips, and with a raspy voice, he said, "I'm thinking about calling it a night."

For conversation sake, Hubert said, "Oh yeah? How're ya getting home?"

Gusto leaned towards his friend, smiled an arrogant smile, and declared: "I'm taking... the *short* way."

"You don't mean—"

"Yes. I'm walking through... *the cemetery!*"

Hubert's checkered teeth were exposed when his mouth flopped open. He couldn't believe what he was hearing. Eyes expanding, he said, "But... but... "

"But what?"

"But the cemetery is haunted!"

Gusto laughed uneasily. "Come on now; I don't believe in that stuff."

"Oh yes you do! Otherwise you would have taken the short way home a long time ago! Everyone in town believes in that stuff, including you!"

"Well... " Gusto's words trailed off as he looked to the floor.

He had to admit, Hubert had a point. Neither of them had walked through the cemetery before now and both men knew why:

the Castle River Graveyard had a bad reputation of being spook central. Everyone for miles around figured the land had turned rotten for some unknown reason, and most folk had a strange story to tell. Still, Gusto was tired of taking the long way home each and every night and tonight he wasn't having it. He was drunk, his hump was aching and feeling extra heavy, and more importantly, his mind was made up. He was taking the short way home no matter what Hubert had to say about the matter, and that was final.

After rolling his right shoulder around in a circle once again, Gusto raked his fingers through his unkempt hair, and said, "I don't believe in that juvenile, ghost-story crapola. Not now. I'm no longer a child, you know. I'm a grown man, for crying out loud. Besides, it's foolish. Don't ya think all that spooky talk is foolish, Hubert? It makes no friggin' sense."

"It ain't foolish!" Hubert said, pleading with every syllable. "It's haunted! The cemetery is bloody *haunted!* Everyone knows *that!*"

Gusto stood up, tossed a few coins on the table, and swallowed back his last swig of ale. He shook his head in mock disgust and said, "Ah, what do *you* know? You're just a crazy old drunk with a shriveled-up arm and a shriveled-up leg. You want to be afraid of the Oogie-Boogie man, be my guest. But don't talk to me about things that go bump in the night 'cause I ain't havin' it. You don't know nothin' 'bout nothin'. An old fool with a line of yellow running down your spine, Hubert—that's what you are. Always have been; always will be."

Now it was Hubert's turn to shake his head in disgust, which he did, saying, "I know enough to stay clear of the cemetery tonight, that's for darn sure... and I ain't no fool. *You're* the fool! Walking through the Castle River Graveyard at this time of night is *insane*, Gusto. It's insane! You need to have your brain examined!"

"Ah, go stick your head in a bucket of donkey shit and tell me what you smell. I'm walking through the cemetery tonight and there ain't an ass-lickin', nose-pickin' thing you can do to stop me."

Gusto slammed his empty mug on the table, lurched towards the door, and staggered outside. He wobbled past a row of horses that were tied to a horse-post, and past the less-than-attractive 'ladies of the evening' that never felt compelled to offer their services to a man like him.

The night was dark and gloomy. A cold wind blew in from the north.

Holding his jacket's lapels in his fist he made his way to the cemetery gates. The weight of his huge hump had him crouched over like Quasimodo. The pain in his back had him rolling his shoulder every few feet. After a nervous pause he stepped through the gateway. He followed the winding path over the roll of a hill and past a row of barren trees. There were graves to the left of him and graves to the right. Some of the tombstones were small while others were large. Some were new but most of the markers were old and weathered by years of abandonment. Statues and sculptures came in all shapes, sizes, and styles. Looking left he saw the Virgin Mary, forever frozen with her arms apart and a sad look carved upon her sculpted face. Looking right he saw a pair of gargoyles, twisted and wicked, endowed with long horns and thick hooves. When he looked towards his feet, which was the majority of the time, he couldn't see anything more than a few dried out leaves blowing across his tattered shoes and the slight outline of the path he was following. When he looked towards the sky, which was no easy task, the moon seemed to smile upon him with a mouth curved like a sickle. And in front of him, in the area he was heading towards, he could see—plain as day—that something wasn't right. There was an object in his path, odd and unusual, taking up a boatload of space. He felt drawn to it.

Gusto staggered faster.

The object began taking shape.

It was a tombstone, a *huge* tombstone—larger than any building in town. It was fifteen stories tall, maybe even twenty. *But how can that be?* Gusto wondered. Anything *that* large would have been sticking out of the Castle River Graveyard like a sore thumb. He would have known about it well before now. He would have *seen* it.

The monolith was impossible. Simply impossible!

As he tried to wrap his senses around the thing that towered over the necropolis the air turned bitter and cold; the wind all but died. Still, he staggered on, over the roll of another hill, towards the gigantic headstone.

Then something incredible happened: a creature - *not of this world* - stepped out from behind the stone column. It stared at Gusto with eyes wide and teeth long. To say the beast was huge would be an understatement. The monster was almost as large as the tombstone itself. It was a hundred feet tall, if not more. It had arms and legs that bulged with muscle and hands designed for crushing. The beast must have weighed a thousand tons.

Looking down at Gusto, the monster said, "**WHAT? IS YOUR NAME?**"

Gusto's chin started quivering, his knees shook, and for a moment he thought he would faint. He said, "Uh… uh… my name?"

"**YES!**"

"Oh my goodness! My name? Why, uh… uh… my name is Gusto!"

"**AND WHERE? DO YOU LIVE?**"

Gusto pointed left; then he changed his mind, shook his head, and pointed right. He started dancing around in one spot with his mouth opening and closing. He was trying to string some words together and having a difficult time achieving his goal. Finally he managed to say: "I live… I live *that* way! Over there, by that store with those things in it! You know the one, don't ya? Boner's, they call it! I live on Humpback Road next to the guy who runs the whorehouse!"

The monster leaned in, breathing hot breath onto Gusto's body. It said, "**AND WHAT? IS THAT! ON YOUR BACK?**"

"My back?"

"**YES!**"

Gusto rolled his shoulder in a circle. His fear made room for his shame and indignity. A tear found life in his eye and he quickly wiped it away. As his line of vision fell towards his feet, he said, "Uh, why… it ain't nothin' special. It's just my hump-a-lump… that's all."

"**YOUR HUMP-A-LUMP?**"

"Yes."

"**GIVE IT TO ME!**"

The monster lowered a massive hand, grabbed Gusto's misshapen back and squeezed. Gusto screamed but that didn't change anything. The monster kept squeezing and squeezing until its work was complete and the hump was ripped from Gusto's body.

Gusto fell to the ground face first, kicking his feet and waving his arms. He figured his head would be pounded into the earth while his guts were splattered in every direction. He cried and begged and when he looked up he was surprised to find that the giant tombstone was gone. The monster was gone, too. Stranger than that, the hump on his back was gone and he was in no pain whatsoever.

For a moment he just laid there, shocked; his eyes were wider than wide.

He rolled his shoulder in a circle and realized that he felt better than he had in twenty-five years. He said, "Well, unleash the chocolate hostages from my backdoor prison! What just happened to me? Where did my hump-a-lump go?"

He reached around and touched his back, but the hump wasn't there. It was gone! He was cured! Somehow—someway—he was cured! There was no blood, no broken bones—his back was in perfect working order. Even his clothing was damage-free.

Gusto jumped to his feet and stood up straight. "Holy beating my trouser snake with my fist of passion," he said. "It's a miracle!"

He ran forward. Then he ran back. Then he ran in a circle: he didn't know what to do. "I've got to tell someone," he said to the empty cemetery. "Oh boy!"

Gusto ran out of the cemetery and returned to the bar as fast he could, which was a hell of a lot faster now than before, thanks to the monster in the graveyard tearing his deformity from his body. When he entered the tavern he was glad to discover that Hubert hadn't left for home yet. He ran to his friend, laughing, crying, and saying, "Hubert! Hubert! It's a miracle!"

Hubert turned. "Gusto… what's going on? Why are you here? Are you all right?"

"Yes! Of course I'm all right! I'm *better* than all right! I'm cured, Hubert! Look! I'm cured!"

Gusto turned, showing Hubert his back.

"Holy jackin' the beanstalk!" Hubert said, astonished. "What happened to your hump?"

"It's gone!"

"I can see that it's gone, but how? Where is it? What happened?"

"I don't know where it is but I know what happened!"

"Well don't just stand there, tell me!"

"I'm trying! I went into the graveyard, right? And I came across this huge tombstone. It must have been a thousand feet tall! And this big monster came out and said, 'Hey little man, what's wrong with your back?' and I told him that I had a hump-a-lump on my back and he said, 'I'll take that' and he snatched it from my body. Can you believe it? *I can't* believe it! He cured me, Hubert! The hump-a-lump is gone! He cured me and then he disappeared!"

Hubert's mind was racing. He said, "That's incredible, Gusto! How do you feel?"

"I feel terrific! I've never felt better!"

"Are you in pain?"

"No!"

"Holy fudge packing honeymooners! If I went into the graveyard, do you think the monster could cure my shriveled-up arm and my shriveled-up leg?"

"I don't see why not! Look at me! I'm perfect now! It's an ass-huffin' miracle!"

"So, the monster is a *good* monster. Is that what you're saying?"

"It sure seems that way to me! Don't you hear what I'm telling you, Hubert? I'm cured!"

Hubert took a good, hard look at his shriveled-up arm and his shriveled-up leg. His heart started pounding in his chest like it was trying to escape. Beads of sweat appeared on his forehead. He said, "Do you think I should go there and... well... you know?"

"Of course I do! You should go to the cemetery right away and look for the huge tombstone. Maybe it'll return. Maybe you'll be cured!"

A moment passed before Hubert released a nervous chuckle. He said, "Well then, what am I waiting for?"

He reached into his pocket, grabbed some change and tossed it onto the table. He waved goodbye to his friend and hobbled out of the bar as fast as he could manage. He made his way past the horses and the prostitutes without giving them a second glance. When he reached the cemetery gates he paused, looked over his shoulder and wondered what to do. Truth was, he didn't *want* to enter the cemetery: it was haunted. Everybody knew *that*. But maybe, he thought, it was haunted in a *good* way. Was *that* possible? Was *that* the situation?

Hubert swallowed back the bulk of his fear, deciding: *Yes. It was possible.*

If Gusto could walk into the cemetery with a hump on his back and walk out of the cemetery with no hump, then it seemed quite possible that *he* could walk into the cemetery with a shriveled-up arm and a shriveled-up leg and walk out of the cemetery with no shrivels.

Hubert closed his eyes and stepped through the gateway, hoping the monster was a nice one.

The night was dark; it was gloomy. A cold wind blew in from the north causing the barren trees to sway. There were graves to the left of him and graves to the right. Some were small and some were large. Looking left he saw the Virgin Mary carved in stone. Looking right he saw gargoyles with long horns and thick hooves. Scattered leaves blew across his shoes as the moon smiled upon him with a mouth shaped like a sickle. And over the roll of a hill, there it was: an object that seemed much too large to be in any necropolis. He felt drawn to it.

Hubert hobbled faster.

The thing standing before him began taking shape.

It was a tombstone, a *huge* tombstone—larger than any building in town.

As his eyes gazed upon the monolith something incredible happened: a creature - *not of this world* - stepped out from behind the stone column, staring down at Hubert with eyes wide and teeth long.

It said, "**WHAT? IS YOUR NAME?**"

Hubert, terrified, said, "Uh… my name?"

"**YES!**"

"Oh sweet butter fingers up my poop shoot! My name? What's my name?"

"**YES!**"

Hubert was so scared that he began slapping himself in the face with his shriveled-up arm. He said, "Uh… my name is Hubert!"

"**AND WHERE? DO YOU LIVE?**"

"Why? Do you want to come to my house and get drunk?"

"**NO! JUST ANSWER THE QUESTION!**"

"Uh… uh… The question?"

"**YES!**"

"Umm… I live at 26 Liverstool Drive. It's a nice place. I've got a shithouse big enough to sleep in and sixteen pigs ready for slaughter. The shithouse has two crunch-holes: one for me, and one for the misses. We can drop a loaf at the same time if the mood strikes us. The shithouse doesn't smell bad, not compared to most. Sometimes it smells kind of nice, like knuckle children on a pillowcase. One of my pigs is pregnant. Her name is Puffy. She's got a—"

"**I DON'T CARE ABOUT YOUR SHITHOUSE *OR* YOUR PIGS!**"

"You don't?"

"**NO!**"

"Oh. Sorry, giant monster. Most of the folk around here are jealous of my shithouse and are fond of pigs. Chickens too."

"**I DON'T LIKE PIGS!**"

"Okay then. Well… now I know. I won't tell you about my pigs, my chickens, or my shitter. Your loss, if you ask me, which of course you didn't—"

"**SHUT UP!**"

"Okay, okay. I'll shut up. But just remember—"

"I'LL REMEMBER WHAT I CHOOSE TO REMEMBER! NOW SHUT THE HELL UP!"

"Well, don't freak out, Tall, Dark and Scary. I'm just trying to be helpful!"

"ANSWER THIS QUESTION BEFORE I SQUISH YOU WITH MY FINGER! WHAT? IS THAT! ON YOUR BACK?"

"My back?"

"YES!"

"Uh... nothing! I don't have anything on my back." Hubert turned. "See? Got nothing there."

The monster leaned in, breathing hot breath onto Hubert's body. It said, **"YOU HAVE NOTHING! ON YOUR BACK?"**

"That's right. Nothing at all!"

"THEN... HERE! HAVE A HUMP!"

(Isn't that just awful? Trust me, I know...)

CURSE OF THE BLIND EEL

The two men stood at the door, looking each other in the eye. Jonathan was terrified; they both were. But Jonathan ignored his fear and put his hand on the doorknob. He twisted his wrist and pushed. The unlocked door opened with a long squeak that sounded like a moan and Jonathan stepped inside.

William grabbed his brother by the shoulder, and said, "Wait."

"No," Jonathan snapped. There was no hesitation in his voice, no uncertainty. William may have been older but Jon was the dominant one, always had been. Plus he was thirty-one now, old enough to appreciate the importance of the situation. "We don't have time to wait. You know that."

"You don't understand.

"Of course I do, you're scared. I get that. I'm scared too. But the sun is coming down and it's coming down fast." He lifted the stake high and cringed as he looked at it, wondering if he'd have the mental strength to pound the tool into a vampire's chest. "If we don't do this soon the Count—"

Lightning cracked and both men turned towards the sound.

The sky was darkening.

"Hold this." Jonathan said. He handed William the wooden spear, reached into his pocket and pulled out a stubby candle. With a long wooden match he lit it and forged ahead.

William reluctantly followed, gripping the stake tightly.

"There!" Jonathan said, pointing at a hallway. "The devil's spawn sleeps down there. At the far end of the hall we'll find a large door that leads to the cellar. We must go now or others shall suffer the same fate as... " Jon's words trailed off. His eyes wavered. He didn't want to think about his wife or his two children. Not again. He wanted to lie to himself and pretend that his family was safe at home, alive—not beheaded and buried in the yard next to the others. Memories of the days past made him tremble.

"But—"

Jonathan focused his thoughts. "But nothing! Give me that!" He snatched the stake from his brother's grasp and handed him the flickering candle. "Hold this and stay close. The cellar is dark and thick with shadow. Night is nearly upon us."

Jonathan walked quickly and his footfalls echoed off the stone walls.

William tried to keep pace but he was having a difficult time; he kept clutching his stomach and crouching.

Jonathan reached the door; turned and said, "Hurry up man! What's taking you?"

William clamped his teeth and approached his brother slowly, like an old man getting ready to die. Then he stopped walking altogether.

"What is it William?"

"I've got…"

"Yes, yes… go on!"

"I need to clip a biscuit.

"What?"

"You heard me. My dumpster keeps opening and a sewer loaf large enough to sit on is threatening to pop out. I've had the back door dribbles for five minutes now and I desperately need to bust a grumpy, lay cable, fire a log on the poop deck. Do you hear what I'm saying, man? I'm ready to chuck the football in my crunch catcher!"

Jonathan rubbed his free hand against his temple. "Oh God, that's not good. Will it hold?"

Lying, William said, "It'll hold."

"Then let us kill the beast as it sleeps. Time is short."

Jonathan dismissed his brother's dilemma and pushed open the large wooden door. He made his way down the stairs two at a time. The men reached the bottom of the staircase, Jonathan first, William a few seconds later. With only one candle between them they saw the coffin together. It was long, black and very old. Silver handles gleamed in the candlelight.

Jon's heart pounded in his chest.

This was it: the moment of truth.

William's ass opened. He thought he was going to snip a yam right there and then. And instead of looking at the coffin he looked at the floor, searching for a suitable place to honey drip the rat.

Jon approached the box, reached into his coat and pulled out a mallet. With the mallet in one hand and the stake in the other, he said, "You open the casket door and I'll pound the stake in deep. After that you're free to do as you wish."

William bit his lower lip, squinted his eyes and nodded his head.

Jonathan, comprehending William's expression, said, "You can fire your rear thrusters into the casket once the abomination is dead, if you so desire."

William forced a smile as he put a hand on the coffin. "Very good. Perhaps I'll drop a sausage down the Count's throat."

Jonathan grinned, "Very well, on the count of three. One! Two! Three!"

William flung open the coffin lid and that was it. He couldn't control his bodily functions any longer. Somehow his brother's counting made things worse, like the counting was for the legless schnauzer squirming from his doghouse, not for the vampire or the coffin lid or anything else that was relevant. And because of this, his ass opened and he began building a log cabin inside his pants.

"Holy green apple splatters," William gasped. "Here comes a sea pickle."

He reached for his crotch with his free hand. His fingers danced around his button and his zipper but luck was not on his side. He was panicking; his fingers were useless. It was like he was trying to remove his trousers with a bushel of bananas. And it was coming. Oh sweet horseshits and hand jobs (*No, not horseshits,* he thought. *Anything but horseshits*), he was getting ready to plunk an ass-goblin into his underwear.

He put the candle on the floor and worked both hands frantically until the button on his pants finally opened. After that, the zipper dropped easy.

He grabbed his belt, slammed his pants to his knees, and squatted. A package of fudge cannonballs snaked from his turd-tunnel and plunked onto the floor. They were long and dense, each the size of a cucumber.

Somewhat relieved, he looked at Jonathan and his mouth dropped open.

The ageless vampire was sitting up, holding Jonathan by the shoulder. Its skin was pale and its eyes were blacker than marbles at the bottom of the ocean.

Jonathan screamed as the vampire knocked the stake away, lurched forward, and bit into his neck. Blood splashed across both faces and Jonathan's hands squeezed into fists.

And when the vampire released his grip, Jonathan didn't fall to the floor like a bundle of rags; he held his ground and turned towards his brother. His teeth grew long. His heart stopped pounding inside his chest. And his flesh—his terrible, terrible flesh—turned a bloodless white, except where the red fluid was smeared and dripping. In those places his skin seemed almost charred.

Jonathan had joined the army of the undead.

"Brother," he said. "Come to me."

A third monstrous corn-eyed butt-snake fell from William's ass and William stood up, holding a forth cattle-cookie inside. With his pants at his ankles, and the biggest pile of fudge-monkeys he had ever unloaded sitting between his feet, he screamed, "Stay back!"

"But why?" Jonathan asked. "Is it not better if I am the one to drink your blood? Joining us is inevitable, and it's not too bad. In fact, I *like* it now. And I'm *hungry*, my brother. *Hungry*. Will you not let me feast? Will you not be my first?"

"No," William cried. "Not you Jonathan! Not you!"

"Yes, me! And there is nothing you can do. So feed me, William. Feed your brother and become one of us! Join us in the brotherhood of eternal life!"

Soulless Jonathan stepped forward and William stepped back as much as he was able, but stepping back was hard. The pants around his ankles restricted his movements, and the meadow muffins he dropped from his crayola box were big enough to trip over.

The Count crept from the coffin and stood beside Jonathan. His teeth were long and white; his eyes were like shiny silver coins. He opened his mouth and released a lengthy high-pitched hiss, and with a reptile voice he said, "Join us, my son. And you shall know the joy of everlasting blood."

The vampire's words made William's skin crawl.

He was in serious trouble; there would be no escape this time. He was too deep in the castle and the night was upon him. The vampires would have their way. Death—or rather, *un*death—seemed inescapable. He needed the hammer and the stake. But the hammer was in his brother's hand and the stake—where was it?

He looked down.

The floor was dark, but he saw something. Perhaps the wooden spear was sitting on the floor in front of him.

He squatted and grabbed it. But it wasn't the stake.

It was a turd.

He stood up, holding the bald-headed ass monkey in his hand like a weapon. "Back!"

Jonathan laughed. "And what do you plan on doing with *that*?"

William didn't know. But he knew one thing: he didn't want to be a vampire. So he said, "You stay back! I mean it! If you don't keep away from me you'll find out what I plan on doing with it!"

The Count said, "There is nothing you can do, my son. So put the bum-brownie down and join us. There is no alternative."

Jonathan moved in. "Drop it my brother. Drop the moose cluster and join us on the other side. Trust me. It's easier this way."

Then it happened: inspiration came, as honest and true as any revelation William had ever known. He knew what to do. It seemed so obvious, so *simple*. A grin crept across his features and he lifted the cattle-cookie high.

"Back off," he said, and this time he sounded like he meant it.

"What are you going to do?"

The Count was nervous now; it was easy to see. He hissed, "It's the curse of the blind eel!"

"This is your last warning," William cautioned. "Back off brother, or I'll make you wish you did."

Jonathan lunged forward with his mouth wide. He was ready to bring his brother into the world of the undead, whether William wanted it or not.

William squeezed the chocolate cigar, creating a root beer float through his fingers. Then he slammed the cooked beans against his neck. The colon cobra smudged along his chin and snicker-bricks bounced off his chest.

His neck was covered.

His fingers were covered.

He rubbed the anus espresso along his face and into his hair, screaming, "OKAY! I'M READY! COME AND GET ME!"

Jonathan stopped his attack.

Horrified, he looked at the Count with his eyes wide and his nose crumpled. He said, "I'm not going to bite him. He's covered in gob-jobbers!"

The Count put a hand to his mouth, looking like he might be sick. "He smells like he's been swimming the brown river for a week!"

"Here's my neck!" William said, arrogantly. "If you don't mind the taste of a toilet turkey, come get a bite!" William extended his neck and stepped towards his attackers.

Both Jonathan and the Count drew back.

"What's a matter? Don't want any? Turtlehead pudding isn't as bad as you think, and I'm right here! I'm *gooooood* eatin'!"

"No," Jonathan said. "I don't want any. I've lost my appetite."

The Count agreed. "You're free to go, and take your rectum warriors with you. Just don't tell others how you escaped or—"

"Or what?"

The count gasped, truly horrified. "Or all of Transylvania will be bathing in bottom barf! Is that what you want?"

William considered the Count's words and decided he was right. Nobody wanted to live in a world where people smeared themselves in clam-crunchies on a nightly basis. So he never told a soul how he escaped, and for that the vampires were grateful.

They never bothered him again.

ABOUT THE AUTHOR

James Roy Daley ~ is a writer, editor, and a professional musician. He studied film at the Toronto Film School, music at Humber College, and English at the University of Toronto. In 2007 his first novel, *The Dead Parade*, was released in 1,110 bookstores across America. In 2009 he founded a book company called *Books of the Dead Press*, where he enjoyed immediate success working with many of the biggest names in horror. His first two anthologies, *Best New Zombie Tales Volume One*, and *Best New Zombie Tales Volume Two*, far exceeded sales predictions, leading many of the top horror writers in the world to view his little company as one worth watching. *13 Drops of Blood* is his first collection. Other novels include *Into Hell*, and *Terror Town*.

Great titles from
BOOKS OF THE DEAD

BEST NEW ZOMBIE TALES (Vol. 1)
BEST NEW ZOMBIE TALES (Vol. 2)
BEST NEW ZOMBIE TALES (Vol. 3)
JAMES ROY DALEY - INTO HELL
JAMES ROY DALEY - 13 DROPS OF BLOOD
JAMES ROY DALEY - THE DEAD PARADE
JAMES ROY DALEY'S - TERROR TOWN
MATT HULTS - ANYTHING CAN BE DANGEROUS
BEST NEW VAMPIRE TALES (Vol. 1)
MATT HULTS - HUSK
CLASSIC VAMPIRE TALES

www.ingramcontent.com/pod-product-compliance
Lightning Source LLC
Chambersburg PA
CBHW030611130626
46552CB00002B/506